Harvest of Hope

Connie Stevens

Heartsong Presents

To my prayer team:
Ann, Diane, Pam, Chris, Ginger,
Tracy, Angela,
and of course, The Posse—Kim, Eileen,
Margie, Darlene, and Kristian.
Thank you for praying me through
the writing of this book.
We serve an awesome God.

A note from the Author:

*I love to hear from my readers! You may correspond with
me by writing:*

Connie Stevens
Author Relations
P.O. Box 9048
Buffalo, NY 14240-9048

ISBN-13: 978-0-373-48619-9

HARVEST OF HOPE

This edition issued by special arrangement with Barbour Publishing,
Inc., 1810 Barbour Drive, Uhrichsville, Ohio, U.S.A.

Chapter 1

Covington Plantation
Near Juniper Springs, Georgia
April 1860

Auralie Covington's heart pounded within her rib cage as she clutched the letter and dashed up the grand staircase with unladylike haste. The pattern of the ornate carpet swam before her, but not from tears of joy. She closed her bedchamber door and stared at her name penned across the front of the letter. The masculine script sent an involuntary chill through her. Perry had never written to her before. In the past, his communications were always sent to Father who told her what he thought she should know. Judging by the rumpled condition of the paper and the water-stained corner, the missive had experienced an arduous journey before reaching the Covington Plantation in the foothills of the north Georgia mountains. Oh, how she prayed the letter didn't say what she dreaded. She took a deep breath and broke the wax seal.

Dear Miss Covington,

"Miss Covington?" Auralie snorted. "We're engaged to be wed and he calls me Miss Covington. What am I to call him? Mr. Bolden?" The irony of her own statement pricked her. Was it not a paradox to feel such trepidation upon receiving a letter from the man she was to marry? Perhaps if the man had been one of her choosing, her emotions wouldn't be in upheaval.

The moisture that had stained the outside of the carefully folded and sealed document blurred the ink in various places within the message, including the date her intended had written it. She glanced over the penned lines that remained unaffected by the water stain.

...leaving London sometime in... If destiny smiles on the ship, the voyage ought not to take more than... I trust your father has impressed upon you the importance of our union. Therefore...

Auralie held the letter closer to the light streaming in the window and squinted, trying to decipher the smeared handwriting. Since she'd been informed four years ago that an agreement joining her in marriage to the son of one of the most powerful landowners in Georgia had been reached, her father had kept her apprised of Perry Bolden's European travels. As long as Bolden remained an entire ocean away, Auralie's apprehension of the arranged unholy wedlock stayed tucked away like a postponed sentence of death. Upon receipt of his letter, however, anxiety exploded through her. The letter echoed the words of her father, leaving no room for doubt that her marriage to Perry Bolden was her duty.

She scanned down the page at the legible parts of the letter. Perry's expectations of her were spelled out like a list of instructions. Between blotches of smeared ink, he described in detail his demands for their engagement soiree, including the names of certain influential people he considered essential to the guest list. Of course, she was to make herself available upon his return to Georgia, and he went so far as to insist she wear a gown of pink silk upon his arrival.

"Pink! I hate pink."

She tossed the letter on her dressing table and parted the lace curtains at the window. The ancient oaks and sweeping willows outside her window wafting in the spring breeze didn't lend their usual calming effect as she bit her bottom lip and twisted the sapphire ring on her right hand. She could no longer pretend the marriage wasn't going to happen. Her destiny was sealed. She now knew how a trapped animal felt.

Her gaze fastened on to a mockingbird perched in the massive oak tree. After it sang through its repertoire, it took flight, making Auralie long to do the same.

"'Oh that I had wings like a dove! for then I would fly away, and be at rest.'"

"Mmm-hmm."

Mammy's soft response caused Auralie to jump as she turned and clapped her hand over her heart. "I didn't hear you come in."

The creases in the face of the ageless black woman deepened. "Them be mighty comfortin' words from our Lawd's Book. Psalm fifty-five, verse six."

Auralie instinctively glanced toward the door that stood ajar. Teaching Mammy to read had been a precious secret between them since she was a child.

Mammy glanced over her shoulder as well. "Ain't nobody creepin' up behind." She gestured to the letter on the dressing table. "That be from Mistuh Bolden, ain't it?"

Auralie picked it up and sighed. "I haven't laid eyes on him since we were children. I can't even remember what he looks like. Mammy, what am I going to do?"

The woman who was more of a loving parent to Auralie than a slave drew her into a tight embrace. "Ah don' know, chile. We's gonna pray on it. My God ain't so weak He be caught by surprise." She set Auralie away from her and cupped her chin. "But right now, yo' fathah want to see you in his study."

Auralie's eyes widened and she clasped her hands together, her fingers working the sapphire ring to and fro. "What does he want? Does he know this letter arrived?"

"Don' know that either, chile, but iffen you keep twistin' on that there ring, you gonna wrench yo' finger off." Mammy patted Auralie's shoulder. "You best be goin', now. Massah Covington don' like to be kep' waitin'."

A tremor quivered through Auralie. If Father demanded to see the letter, she'd have no choice but to hand it over.

The morning rays filtered through the trees and sparkled off the dew that still clung to the grass. Auralie gathered her billowing yellow skirt and stepped into the carriage, Mammy close at her heels. After Father had blustered about the illegible, water-stained parts of Perry's letter yesterday, he'd admonished Auralie to ready herself for the man's return to the States. If she had to endure one more lecture about Perry's extensive European education, his family's money, or the honor he'd bestowed on her by consenting to the marriage arrangement, she'd surely be ill. But a smile tweaked her lips when she recalled how she'd nodded in feigned agreement to everything her father had said and then asked permission to visit the dressmaker in Juniper Springs to commission three new gowns. Father had mumbled something about looking her best and waved her away in dismissal.

The carriage pulled away, and Mammy leaned slightly forward, her black eyes twinkling. "Yo' gonna have the dressmaker sew you up a pink silk gown?"

Auralie pressed her lips together and sent Mammy an exasperated look. "You read Perry's letter!"

"'Course I did. You lef' it on yo' bed table las' night. An' since when you and me kep' secrets from each other?" Deep dimples of amusement sank into Mammy's cheeks.

Auralie could never be annoyed with Mammy. The woman protected her heart like a precious thing hidden away in her pocket. "Never." She shrugged. "And I'm *not* ordering a pink gown. I don't care what that letter says."

They rode in silence for a time. After a few miles, the playful expression returned to Mammy's eyes. "Ah hear'd yo' mama talkin' with yo' brother's intended."

Auralie's older brother, Dale, and his fiancée, Gwendolyn, had announced their wedding date months ago. Gwendolyn and her mother had visited Covington Plantation on a few occasions to discuss wedding plans with Auralie's mother. It was apparent that her soon-to-be sister-in-law was much more eager to become a Covington than Auralie was to become a Bolden.

Mammy broke into her reverie. "I hear her say she havin' six bridesmaids. Mmm, gonna be some fancy doin's. She showed yo' mama swatches o' cloth for the dresses, and ever'one of 'em was pink."

"No!" Auralie stabbed the floor of the carriage with her yellow parasol.

Mammy slapped her knees and threw her head back with a deep-throated chortle. "Yo' gonna wear pink one way or the other."

The knot in Colton Danfield's stomach tightened the way it always did when he prepared to go to town and leave Barnabas working alone. He swept his gaze across the field all the way to the tree line. Even though Barnabas was no longer a slave, Colton wasn't so naive as to believe a slave catcher who thought Barnabas might be worth a bounty wouldn't try to take him, despite the paper he carried in his shirt pocket.

The law stated Colton was expected to see to it that Barnabas left the state upon being freed, but Barnabas rejected the idea. Colton could still hear the man's impassioned plea.

"Please don' make me leave you, Mistah Colton. Dem bounty hunters search fo' ever' colored man who travel no'th, free or not. I's gettin' too old to run from dem dogs. Let me make my mark on a paper sayin' I workin' fo' you. Dat's what I want to do. Please, Mistah Colton..."

The memory made Colton smile. He'd written up an indenture agreement, read it to Barnabas, and let him make his mark, just to keep everything legal. But in Colton's heart, the man was an employee and friend. He slept in the lean-to behind the cabin, and Colton paid him a wage. Even after four years, Barnabas's eyes glistened every month when Colton placed eight gold coins in his work-scarred hand.

Colton slipped his arms into the black wool coat Pastor Winslow had given him. Though slightly too large for Colton, he didn't care. The coat, given to the pastor by a parishioner, was the only garment of fine quality the old preacher ever owned. The elderly saint had precious little to his name when he died, other than the forty acres and small herd of sheep, all of which he'd bequeathed to Colton. Over the past four years, Colton had made a few improvements as he was able and was pleased with the way his corn crop was growing and with the number of spring lambs that frolicked in the pasture. But Colton would give it all back in a moment if it meant sitting with Pastor Winslow one more time and gleaning nuggets of wisdom from the dear old man.

He ran his fingers over the well-tailored sleeve and smiled with remembrance. How he missed his friend and mentor.

Colton glanced at the position of the sun. If he didn't get moving, he'd miss the meeting at Maybelle's Café in town this morning. No doubt much of the debate would center on the upcoming election. While Colton wasn't overly vocal about his opinions, this morning was different. Jack McCaffey, the owner and publisher of the *Juniper Springs Sentinel*, had asked Colton to speak on behalf of the area farmers. Joseph E. Brown, the current governor, had yet to take a stand one way or the other regarding secession, but Colton had serious doubts about the scruples and ethics of Shelby Covington, the man running against Governor Brown.

He saddled his horse, Jasper, and led the animal out to the edge of the cornfield where Barnabas worked. The former slave straightened and sent Colton a grin.

"You must be fixin' to go to town. You's wearin' the preacher's coat."

Colton smiled and nodded. He normally saved the fine garment for going to church, but he hoped wearing Pastor Winslow's black worsted might rub a bit of the preacher's sage insight onto him before he spoke at the meeting.

He pointed to the far side of the cornfield. "What do

you think? Should we wait another week before planting the other half?"

Barnabas raised his hand and shaded his eyes. "Yes suh, that be about right. This here first plantin' oughta be over a foot tall by then."

Colton turned and glanced across the footpath from the cornfield where a black-and-white dog sat in the shade of the pin oaks and kept vigil over the three dozen sheep and another dozen lambs. Colton turned to look over his shoulder at Barnabas. "I have to admit you were right about getting a dog to help watch the sheep. He's been worth every penny."

The presence of the dog also eased Colton's mind somewhat when he had to leave Barnabas alone on the place, knowing the animal would bark if he picked up the scent of any strangers nosing around. It always made Colton smile when he remembered the day he brought the pup home and let Barnabas name him. "Freedom," he'd said. And from that day on, they called the dog Freedom, or Free for short.

Colton hoped to one day acquire more land, expand the flock, and plant more acreage, but not until he could afford to pay another man to help work it. It pleased him to pay Barnabas a wage, even if it did mean they ate beans and salt pork most days. The corn crop looked good, and his herd of sheep had doubled in size. The future held promise, but only with God's blessings.

Barnabas dragged his faded sleeve across his forehead. "Mistah Colton, you gots any plans fo' gittin' yo'self hitched?"

"What?" Colton shook his head, certain he'd misunderstood.

Barnabas grinned and his eyes danced. "Iffen you was to marry and have yo'self a passel o' sons, you and me could set on the porch in a couple o' rockin' chairs while the young'uns worked the field."

Colton snorted. "Marriage is a long ways off for me. If God wants me to marry, He's going to have to put the woman right in front of me so I trip over her."

Colton put his foot in the stirrup and swung into the saddle, but tugged the reins to hold Jasper in place. "Barnabas, do you have—"

Barnabas patted his shirt pocket where the paper declaring him a free man lay folded and tucked. "Right here, Mistah Colton, jus' like always."

An uneasy smile stretched Colton's face as he returned Barnabas's wave. He bumped his heels against Jasper's flanks and pulled his thoughts back to the meeting being held at Maybelle's Café. In addition to the speculation over the governor's race, the topic of secession had several folks engaged in hot debate. None of the landowners attending today's meeting used slaves, and most of them, like Colton, had farms under a hundred acres. The wealthy and powerful plantation owners whose holdings were vastly larger than Colton's claimed they couldn't turn a profit without slaves. That philosophy always soured Colton's stomach.

The town of Juniper Springs came into view. He reined in the chestnut gelding and dismounted, taking note of the men headed in the direction of Maybelle's Cafe. Colton knew most of them and didn't see anyone who stood out as suspicious. The last thing they needed was someone carrying information back to the plantation owners.

He stepped aside to let a young woman in a sweeping yellow dress with a matching parasol pass. The older Negro woman with her scowled at Colton, as if she considered him a threat to the lovely young woman in front of her. He tipped his hat and mumbled a good morning, moving on to the door of the café.

A lively discussion was already underway when Colton stepped inside. Maybelle Gooch, proprietor of the café, put a cup of coffee in his hand the moment he entered. He gave the plump, middle-aged woman a smile and a nod of thanks, and made his way to a table already occupied by two other men. As Colton listened to the speakers, most agreed on the immorality of slavery and thought secession was a bad idea. Colton took the floor and presented the position of the farmers with small acreage, the most pressing issue being how to protect their properties in the event the politicians in Atlanta voted to secede and war came to their part of the country.

Several of the attendees called out their agreement as he made his way back to his seat.

"I'm with you, Colton."

Another added, "Colton knows what he's talking about."

Slight movement of yellow near the entrance caught Colton's attention. The same woman he'd passed on the boardwalk stood just inside the door, listening intently. Judging by her attire, she was from a wealthy family, and if the Negro woman with her was an indication, her family owned slaves.

Colton fixed his eyes on the woman in yellow. What was she doing here? Did she plan to take a list of names of the attendees back to her fancy home? At that moment, the woman's eyes met his and his breath caught. Something flickered across her face, as though she recognized him. But Colton had never seen her before in his life. If he had, he'd remember a woman as beautiful as this one.

The door opened and two more men shuffled in, blocking Colton's view. When the men moved, the woman was gone. But what information might she divulge? He rose, hoping to see which way she went.

Chapter 2

Needles of panic spurred Auralie from the café where she'd merely stopped for something cool to drink. How was she to know she'd stumbled upon some kind of political meeting? Distracted over the arrival of Perry Bolden's letter, she was completely taken by surprise when she heard some of the men call him by name.

Confused thoughts raced through her mind. How did he arrive back in the States so soon? Had he traveled on the same ship with his letter? And why was Perry attending such a meeting? When she realized she'd just stared into the face of the man whose return she dreaded, the blood in her veins turned to ice. All she wanted to do was hide behind her parasol and set her feet to flying as fast as she could run. She shoved the questions away and allowed flustered confusion to carry her out the door.

The parasol resisted her effort to thrust it open, and the horrid thing took on a mind of its own. She gave it one more hard yank, and it leaped from her grip like a rock from a slingshot. A man on the boardwalk made his acquaintance with the cantankerous thing when it propelled itself into his stomach.

"Oof!" He doubled over and grabbed his middle, gasping like he'd just run uphill.

To Auralie's further mortification, the poor man fell forward just as she bent to retrieve the parasol, and he tripped over her, sending her sprawling across the boardwalk in a most unladylike fashion.

With a groan that sounded like a strangled cat, the gentleman untangled his arms from hers and scrambled upright. Flames rushed up Auralie's throat and into her face. Her stomach twisted into a knot. From her face-down position on the boardwalk she could hear Mammy sputtering close by. But the hands that reached down to cup her elbows and help her stand weren't Mammy's. They were strong, calloused hands. Masculine hands. White hands.

Once she was steady on her feet, the man released his grip on her arms and proceeded to retrieve his hat and brush dust off his finely-tailored coat.

She sucked in a breath and whisked an errant curl away from her face before raising her eyes to meet his.

It was him.

While he continued to wheeze air in and out as he clutched his hat, mahogany eyes arrested her and she froze in place. She'd tried a hundred times to remember what Perry Bolden looked like as a child. Were his eyes this dark? Was his hair the color of walnuts? She certainly didn't remember him being this devastatingly handsome. But then, he was only fourteen years old, and she eleven, the last time she recalled seeing him. She opened her mouth, but the only sound that emerged was an undignified squeak.

"Now see what you done?" Mammy sent a venomous

look at Bolden before fluttering like a mother hen over her. "You all right, honey girl?"

Auralie tried to snatch her composure and stuff it back into place. She cleared her throat and begged God to give her coherent words to speak to this man who stood before her. But he spoke first.

"I'm terribly sorry, miss. Please forgive me. I hope you are unhurt."

Her throat tightened like it was trussed up in a corset. Ever since his letter had arrived yesterday, she'd tried to imagine what she might say when she faced her fiancé for the first time. Nothing she'd learned from Miss Josephine Westbrook at the Rose Hill Female Academy came to mind. She commanded her scrambled thoughts back into some semblance of order.

"Ah, yes…I'm unharmed." Finally. A lucid thought.

Mammy fussed for a few more moments, and Auralie used the time to regain her poise. She fixed her feet in place and refused to allow them the freedom to do as they pleased, which was to flee in the opposite direction. But no amount of finishing school training or memories of Miss Westbrook's prim examples could curtail the angst that twisted through her over Perry's arrival. She'd barely had time to digest the implications of his rumpled letter tucked under her handkerchief box in her bureau drawer. Couldn't God have at least given her a couple of weeks to get used to the idea? She shrugged off the plea. She'd had four years to get used to the idea, but the arranged betrothal appealed to her even less today than it had on her sixteenth birthday when her father announced it. She disciplined her lungs to draw a slow, even breath and then discreetly release it.

"I, too, apologize, Mr. Bolden." Had her father orches-trated this encounter, he'd have her strike an aristocratic pose of resplendent grace and reply with demure dignity. No such formalities fell within her grasp at the moment, so she merely lifted her chin. "I had imagined our first meeting would take place under much different circumstances. I only received your letter yesterday, and as you can imagine, we haven't had time to prepare for your arrival. My father will be pleased that you're here of course. I suppose you will be coming by the house to finalize the terms of the agreement."

The man's eyebrows dipped and he shook his head, puzzlement etching lines into his features. "You must have me confused with someone else, miss. My name isn't Bolden. It's Danfield. Colton Danfield." He drew his hat up over his heart in a gentlemanly gesture.

Auralie blinked and her heart paused before resuming its erratic tapping. While embarrassment still heated her face, wilting relief coursed through her—a bewildering duet of emotions. Her knees wobbled as the tension drained from her and reprieve took its place. She started to flap her hand in front of her face, but genteel restraint curled her fingers closed and she returned her hand to hide within the sunny folds of her skirt.

"Oh my. It does seem as though I've made an error." How she wished she had a fan in her possession to obstruct Mr. Danfield's view of her fiery countenance. She didn't dare give her parasol another opportunity to inflict further damage. "In addition to nearly skewering you with my parasol, I've compounded the insult by assuming you were someone else. Dear me, do accept my apology, Mr. Danfield."

A slow, polite smile stretched Mr. Danfield's lips and he gave a slight bow. "Think nothing of it, Miss…"

"Covington. Miss Auralie Covington." She extended her hand, which he took and held for the briefest of moments.

* * *

Covington? Surely she wasn't…

"Of the Covington Plantation?"

Her light brown hair reflected the sun, and the curl she kept pushing back tumbled again when she nodded. "That's right."

Shelby Covington's daughter?

Cautionary flags waved in his brain. He'd noticed her standing by the café door long enough to hear much of what was said, but he mustn't allow his imagination to run rampant. Still, it was entirely possible she'd been sent to spy and report back to her father the names of those in attendance at the meeting. After all, who would suspect a lovely young woman with her mammy in tow?

Shelby Covington would like nothing better than to bully the area farmers into deference to his ambitions. Small farmers may not have the money or power the larger plantation owners did, but each one still had a vote. Covington's ability to gain votes in exchange for political favors might work in wealthier circles, but for those farmers who had to sweat and scratch to eke out a living, money might sway people to cast a ballot for a man with whom they otherwise had no affinity. Colton hoped he was wrong about Miss Covington's reason for being at the meeting, but for the moment, he couldn't think why a refined young woman would patronize Maybelle's Café.

Maybelle's place was clean, but the furnishings were plain, and she served tasty, but simple fare. It wasn't the kind of place Colton expected to see a person of wealth.

He switched his hat from one hand to the other and gave her a polite nod, guarding his words and measuring her reaction. "I see." *Careful.* "The news of your father's run for the governor's seat is all over town."

After the initial humiliating encounter, Miss Covington

now appeared to have a tight grip on her dignity, but she didn't resort to batting her eyelashes or employing flirtatious coyness. His level of respect increased a notch.

She looked him straight in the eye. "Father doesn't discuss such matters around me or my mother. Perhaps I'll buy a newspaper after I visit the dressmaker so I can read about my father's political ambitions."

The young woman's statement surprised Colton, and he would have pursued the subject, but at that moment the older black woman who accompanied her continued her solicitous care of Miss Covington.

"Miss Auralie, iffen we don't hurry, you gonna be late fo' yo' appointment with the dressmaker." The old slave woman cast a defensive, sideways look at him.

"But I don't have—" Miss Covington pressed her lips closed for a moment. "It's all right, Mammy. Why don't you go along and tell Mrs. Hyatt I'll be there in a moment."

The woman shifted a distrustful scowl in Colton's direction. She reminded him of a ruffled hen guarding her chicks. He half expected her to flap her arms at him to hold him at bay, and he bit his lip to keep from grinning. She tossed one more treacherous glare at Colton and turned to Miss Covington. "I be waitin' fo' you outside the dressmaker's door. You call out iffen you need me." With that, she huffed her way down the boardwalk.

Miss Covington wiggled the mechanism on her parasol up and down a few times. Colton took a half step backward and eyed the frilly contraption warily as it finally whooshed open. He wondered if Miss Covington consciously clutched the thing like a shield or if perhaps it was only his imagination.

She'd not mentioned some of the uncomplimentary comments made about her father in the meeting, but she must have heard them. How could she be unaware of the questionable tactics and special favors her father employed to gain support of wealthy, influential people?

He pasted a smile in place and steered the conversation in another direction. "The name Bolden—were you referring to the Boldens at Ivywood Plantation?"

A flicker of something akin to alarm blinked across her face. No doubt she regretted mistaking Colton's identity, but he suspected something more. There were rumors afoot that the Bolden clan was backing Shelby Covington for governor. Since she professed to not knowing anything about her father's plans, would she deny knowledge of her father's connection with the Boldens?

She lifted the parasol over her head and shaded her face.

"The Boldens have been friends with my family for as long as I can remember. Before I was born, actually." Her gaze darted about like a wren seeking a safe branch on which to perch. Was that a tremor in her voice?

It seemed to Colton if the Boldens were old family friends, wouldn't she know them on sight? Why would she mistake him for a Bolden? His curiosity piqued, but she took several tiny side steps and twirled her parasol.

"If you'll excuse me, Mr. Danfield. I really must be going. Good day."

He placed his hat on his head and tugged the brim as she stepped gracefully down the boardwalk in the direction of the dressmaker's shop. It wasn't polite to stare, but Colton couldn't tear his eyes away from the retreating figure of Auralie Covington. Her father's political ambitions weren't the only reason for the bad taste in his mouth. Shelby Covington was also the man from whom Colton had bought Barnabas. The cruelty Barnabas had endured at Covington Plantation was evident from the scars carved by the whip on his back and shackles on his legs. Colton gritted his teeth. Only a man devoid of common sense would be attracted to the lovely Miss Covington, given the differences in their backgrounds. But fascination overrode the warnings.

Auralie ran her hand over several samples of material the dressmaker showed her. Despite Frances Hyatt's attempts to convince her pink would bring out the roses in her cheeks, Auralie adamantly refused to consider the color, rejecting anything that remotely resembled Perry Bolden's instructions. Instead, she selected a sapphire blue lawn with ivory trim for a morning dress and a mossy green satin for a new dinner gown.

"What you goin' to pick for when Mistah Bolden come to meet you?" Mammy's eyes twinkled as she fingered a pale pink silk.

Auralie sighed. A sinking sensation weighted her stomach, taunting her with anticipation of the inevitable. Still, she retained enough rebelliousness to shove aside the pink. The array of fabrics spread across the dressmaker's worktable rivaled the colors in the most meticulously tended garden. She reached past the pink and grasped a bolt of royal purple taffeta.

"Wouldn't this be lovely with orchid embroidery along the neckline?"

Mrs. Hyatt beamed. "You do have an eye for quality, Miss Covington. That's an excellent piece of goods." She unrolled a length and draped it across Auralie's shoulder, letting it cascade down in front of her. "Oh my, it's exquisite. You will look like a princess in this gown." The woman's loosely pinned, gray bun flopped from side to side as she cocked her head one way and then another.

"I think so, too." Defiance tickled Auralie's stomach, and she pulled her lips into a smile. "I also like that tiny lavender floral for a morning gown."

The dressmaker opened one fold of the material. "Instead of the blue lawn?"

"No." Auralie picked up the corner of the fabric and held it against her. "In addition to the blue. Would you have any eyelet lace to edge it?"

"Indeed I do." The woman bustled back and forth to her storeroom, bringing out a number of trims for Auralie's approval. "This cloth is so springlike. It will look lovely, my dear. So, that is a total of four dresses." Delight tinkled in Mrs. Hyatt's tone, and the woman scurried to gather her pencil and order book.

Mammy sidled up close to Auralie's shoulder. "Honey girl, yo' fathah agreed to three."

"I know, Mammy." Her gaze locked with Mammy's warm chocolate brown eyes, knowing the dear woman would understand what Auralie couldn't speak. "My choices are slipping away from my grasp. I doubt Father will even notice that I have four new dresses instead of only three."

"He be noticin' when he got to pay the bill." No scolding edged Mammy's tone, but Auralie detected a hint of sympathy.

With a small shake of her head, Auralie curled her fingers around Mammy's. "He might bluster awhile, but I'll remind him that he said I was to look my best." The very idea of primping and preening for Perry Bolden twisted her stomach into a knot. "Who knows how much longer I'll be free to make my own decisions about what dress to wear or which color looks best on me? I realize I'm only feeding my own vanity, but in a few months I may not have a choice."

Her throat tightened, and the lavender print of the material she still held blurred in her hands, but she refused to give in to tears. Her father might have intimidated her mother into submission, he may have stolen his only daughter's privilege of choice, but she'd not let him rob her of her grace. She blinked back the burning in her eyes and forced a smile. For now, she'd grasp whatever freedom was within her reach and relish it.

Chapter 3

The aroma of freshly brewed coffee wafted up the stairs to greet Auralie when Mammy came to awaken her, but Auralie had been up for hours. Every time she closed her eyes, images of Colton Danfield wouldn't let her rest. While relief had skittered down her spine yesterday when she realized it wasn't Perry Bolden to whom she spoke, she never conceived meeting a man like Colton Danfield could linger in the recesses of her mind to such a degree as to interrupt her sleep.

She stepped away from the open window and clutched the edges of her dressing gown, wrapping it around herself against the cool morning air as Mammy plunked the tray containing coffee and cinnamon toast down on the tea table.

Mammy clucked her tongue and waddled across the room. "Honey girl, what you doin' standin' there breathin' in that chilly air. You's goin' to catch the grippe. Now come on away from there." She shut the window and nudged Auralie over to the chair upholstered in rich tapestry roses. "Here now, you drink this coffee and warm yo'self. What you doin' up so early anyway?"

Auralie took a sip of the steaming brew. "I can't get that man out of my mind."

"What man? You frettin' over Mistah Bolden comin'?"

"No. Well, yes, I am, but that's not the man I'm talking about." She nibbled on the cinnamon toast. "That man I met yesterday in town, Mr. Danfield—"

"You mean dat man who knocked you down? I wanted to kick him right in the shinbone. Who do he think he is, bargin' out the door thataway and tramplin' my honey girl?" Mammy snorted her displeasure. "He oughta be put in jail till the sun don't shine no mo', that's what."

Auralie patted Mammy's hand. "It's all right, he apologized. He didn't mean any harm."

"Hmph." Mammy muttered under her breath and began brushing Auralie's hair.

The recurring picture of Mr. Danfield bent over and holding his stomach filled Auralie's face with heat. "I've never been so embarrassed. I nearly ran him through with my parasol. The poor man."

Mammy harrumphed again as she deftly twisted, curled, and pinned each lock of Auralie's hair. "Po' man! I'd like to give that po' man a piece o' my mind. A proper young lady ain't even safe walking down the street with men like him crashin' through doors."

Auralie suppressed a giggle. If she'd let Mammy have her way, Mr. Danfield might be the one in mortal danger. Other than the initial chagrin over the awkward encounter, the one thing that continued to niggle at Auralie was the way Mr. Danfield regarded her with an air of contempt. Something in his tone and demeanor bespoke disapproval, but she didn't think it had anything to do with their collision. She pushed the thought aside as she listened to Mammy's prattle.

"Glad he had the good manners to 'pologize and tip his hat, but I don't mind tellin' you I weren't comf'table leavin' you standin' there with him while I went on ahead to the dressmaker's." She leaned this way and that peering at her handiwork. "Leastways he *not* Mistah Bolden."

"He asked what my connection was with the Bolden family. I hardly knew what to tell him." Auralie finished her toast and took another sip of coffee.

"Why he ask that?" Mammy put the finishing touches on Auralie's hair and turned toward the wardrobe.

She stood and let her dressing gown slip off her arms. "He was speaking in that meeting and some of the other men called out to him. I thought they said *Bolden*, but there were so many people talking and so much noise, I must not have heard them correctly. Now I understand they were calling him by his given name, Colton. But at the time, I panicked. I thought Perry had arrived, and all I wanted to do was run away. When we collided on the sidewalk, I called him Mr. Bolden."

Mammy helped her step into her hooped petticoat, adjusted the stays, and tied the satin strings. "So what you tell him when he ask about the Boldens?"

Auralie pushed out her breath as Mammy laced her corset. "I just told him the Boldens were old friends of the family." She turned and faced the mirror, watching Mammy's animated expression in reaction to her statement.

"You didn't tell him you was engaged to Mistah Perry?"

Auralie shook her head, her face warming. "It hasn't been formally announced yet, so I'm not obligated to tell anyone. I never met Mr. Danfield until yesterday, so it was hardly any of his business."

Mammy's arched eyebrows said more than her silence

as she fastened the long row of buttons down the back of Auralie's morning dress.

Curiosity itched her sense of discretion and she longed to scratch it. "Mammy, what do you suppose he was doing at that meeting?"

A low chortle rumbled from Mammy's throat. "Doin' what men do. Talkin' and talkin' and not makin' much sense. 'Sides, didn' you say it was some kind o' political meetin'? Best you ask yo' fathah 'bout that, but ain't likely he'll be tellin' you nuthin'. He always say he want his women to be beautiful, and dat's all."

His women, indeed. Frustration competed with her curiosity. "I can't understand how Mother can sit to one side, doing nothing but being beautiful, like some kind of—*ornament.* Why do men assume women have no ability to think for themselves or contribute something to society? I want to be more than that. I just wish I knew what it is that I truly want."

She released a sigh and wished some of her vexation could leak away with it. "What's so wrong with asking questions? How am I supposed to learn about the events that might steer us toward secession? I know my father holds some strong opinions about it, but he doesn't speak of it in front of me."

"Mmm-hmm." Mammy's tone warned her she was treading too close to the firmly established line that divided the sexes. "You best watch yo' words. Massah Covington not like it iffen he know you sayin' such things, 'specially to me."

"And to whom should I say them?"

Mammy's fingers paused halfway up the back of Auralie's dress. "Honey girl, this here be yo' twentieth spring. You stopped needin' a mammy a long time ago." Her voice grew thick and husky. "You couldn't be mo' dear to me if you was my own chile. The secret place in my heart is glad when you talk to me like a baby girl with her mama. But darlin', yo' gots to remember I ain't nuthin' but a slave, and yo' mama is a refined mistress of the house."

Auralie turned and slipped her arms around Mammy's neck and sighed. "But I can't talk to Mother the way I can talk to you. When I try to draw her into conversation about what's going on in the South, she shushes me and says it's not appropriate for a proper lady to discuss such things."

Mammy cupped both hands on Auralie's cheeks and placed a kiss on her forehead, then turned her around and continued buttoning the dress up to Auralie's slumped shoulders.

"Mother tells me Perry would disapprove if I persist in expressing opinions about things that don't concern me." She blew out an exasperated breath. "I don't care what Perry thinks. Every night I pray God will help me find some way out of this arranged marriage."

She whirled to face Mammy again. "Marrying Perry would be like marrying a complete stranger. I'd rather marry the man who collided with me yesterday."

"Here, now. You keep jumpin' around like dat and I'm likely to get yo' buttons in the wrong buttonholes." Mammy finished the buttons and fastened an ivory lace collar to the peach-colored dress.

Auralie stood still a moment longer. "Mr. Danfield spoke at that meeting, and I heard some of the men there say Father was a man of questionable ethics. At first it made me angry to hear it, but deep in my heart—" She lowered herself to the tapestry chair. "I wonder if they may be right. Does it make me a terrible daughter to question my father's honor?"

Mammy stooped to button Auralie's shoes. "You stop

that talk now. You might be headstrong, but terrible is somethin' you never be."

"I stood in the doorway of that café yesterday long enough to hear they were talking about secession and how it would bring hardship on many people. They debated over the upcoming elections and most of the men in attendance believed Father wouldn't make a good governor. I never realized how secession could hurt some of the smaller farmers." She propped her elbow on the arm of the chair and leaned her chin on her hand. "I think Father is for secession because he wants to continue using slaves."

She reached down and grasped Mammy's hands, halting their task. "I never thought much about it before, but here I am, old enough now to take care of myself, but you still have to bring me my breakfast and dress me. You aren't free to do as you please."

"What make you think I ain't pleased to tend to you every day?"

A soft smile tipped Auralie's lips. "I know your heart, and you do everything with love. I just wish you had a choice."

Mammy shook her head. "No sense in wishin' for somethin' that ain't never gonna be. Now prayin' for God to help you find a way out of dis here arranged marriage? Dat be somethin' else. We sure can pray, 'cause I don' want my honey girl to be anything but happy."

"Mammy?"

"Hmm?"

"Do you think God cares about us being happy?"

Mammy jerked upright and plopped her hands on her ample hips. "Well, 'course He do. Why you even ask such a question?"

Auralie lifted her shoulders. "Just look around. You and those like you don't want to be bound in slavery, but you are. If God is my heavenly Father, is He as domineering as my father who sits behind his desk in his study?"

The lines across Mammy's forehead smoothed out and she picked up the Bible that lay on Auralie's bedside table. Her thick fingers wandered through the pages until she found the place she sought. Auralie's gaze followed Mammy's quick glance toward the door. It was shut tight. Mammy began to read.

"I will say of the Lawd, He my refuge and my fo'tress; my God, *in Him* will I trust." She ran her finger further down the page. "Because he hath set his love upon Me, therefo' will I deliver him; I will set him on high, because he know my name. He call on me, and I will answer him; I be with him in trouble." She lowered the book. "Do that sound like a heavenly Father who don't care 'bout His chillun?" She replaced the Bible on the nightstand and took Auralie's hands in hers.

"Honey girl, God's Word say if you love Him, He know your name, and He promise to hear you and be with you, no matter what kind o' trouble you be goin' through. Dat's the kind o' heavenly Father we have."

Colton wrangled a bleating ewe from a patch of blackberry vines into which she'd gotten herself entangled. Without so much as an appreciative *baa,* she ambled back to join the rest of the flock.

Colton pulled off his gloves and dragged his sleeve across his forehead. "We probably ought to chop down these thorny vines so the sheep don't get caught again."

"No suh!" Barnabas shook his head. "Dem vines give some o' the sweetest blackberries in the summer." He smacked his lips. "Make my mouth water jus' thinkin' 'bout it. Blackberries make a mighty fine cobbler."

Colton grinned and relented. "All right, but it'll be your job to keep the sheep out of the vines."

"Sheeps must be th' dumbest animals God evah created." Barnabas declared as he helped Colton and Free herd the woolies toward the small barn. Without the dog's help, the chore might've taken the two men half the morning.

"Put the lambs in that far pen." Colton pointed. "Once we start the shearing, we'll do the young ones last and keep their wool separate."

When they had all the critters corralled, Colton grabbed the horns of one of the young rams and steered the 125-pound animal toward the shearing stall. As the two men worked together, Barnabas plied Colton with questions about the sheep. Having been a field hand most of his life, working with sheep filled the former slave with fascination.

"Mistuh Colton, how come dees sheeps don't have no wool on da faces or underbellies?"

After watching Barnabas emerge from his shell of oppression and submission into a man who glowed joy and wonder, Colton didn't mind answering his friend's endless questions as they clipped the valuable wool and gathered it into burlap sacks.

"These are Gulf Coast sheep, and they are bred especially to thrive in the heat here in the south. Their wool is finer than the sheep raised in the north because the breed was developed with Spanish Merino sheep. The finer wool and not having any wool on their faces, legs, and bellies helps them adapt to hot weather and humidity in this area of the country."

Barnabas clipped the last of the wool from the ram and turned it loose in the pen. The sheep bleated its indignation, and then trotted over to shove its face into the feeding trough.

Barnabas snagged the next candidate and guided it into the shearing stall. "You learn all dat from da preacher?"

"Mm hm." The question stirred Colton's heart. He'd learned that and so much more from the man he considered his mentor. He wished Pastor Winslow could lend him wise counsel regarding the young woman with whom he'd collided a few days ago. His inability to get Auralie Covington out of his mind disconcerted him.

"What you thinkin' on so hard?" Barnabas's voice interrupted his thoughts.

Colton bent over another sheep and began shearing. "I met a young woman in town the other day."

Barnabas's dark face split with a wide grin. "Dat so?"

"It's not what you're thinking." Colton shoved a pile of wool to one side and continued working. "This girl is Shelby Covington's daughter."

At the mention of Covington's name, Barnabas halted mid-task and their gazes connected. After years of living on the Covington Plantation, the former slave no doubt had vivid memories of the cruelty he'd endured at the hands of Shelby Covington and his overseers. Painful memories engraved their marks in Barnabas's eyes, prompting Colton's stomach to tighten. Once again, gratitude spilled over Colton's heart for God allowing him the opportunity to purchase his friend's freedom.

Barnabas squatted and quietly returned to work, stuffing wool into the burlap sacks. "I recall he had a daughter. Long time ago, I 'member her—she couldn't've been more'n eleven or twelve years old—she used to come sneakin' down to Slave Row with a basket. She give cookies and fruit to the chilluns, sometime she even play with the younger ones." He leaned back on his heels and stared at the barn roof like the memory was painted there.

"She used to bring storybooks, and some of the li'l col-

ored chilluns would sit with her and she showed dem words
in the books." He looked Colton in the eye and lowered his
voice, even though there was nobody to overhear except
the sheep. "She taught a lot o' dem chilluns to read...."
He lowered his gaze. "Till the day the overseer caught her
and take her to her daddy. After dat, I don' 'member seein'
her no more. Heard she went off to a school somewheres."

Shelby Covington's daughter taught slave children to
read? Colton could only imagine what her father must have
thought about that. This new revelation gave him pause.
He'd assumed Miss Covington was a pampered, indulged
young woman who cared for nobody but herself. Perhaps
he'd judged her too quickly. True, she'd been accompanied
by her maid, but the slave was obviously owned by Shelby
Covington and as such was obliged to do his bidding.

What Colton couldn't figure out was why Miss Covington seemed so relieved to learn his name wasn't Bolden,
and why alarm flickered through her eyes when he asked
about her connection with the Bolden clan.

Even more bewildering was why the memory of his encounter with Auralie Covington pervaded his senses and
refused to leave him alone. He had no answer other than
his initial wariness of her taking information to her father.
But in the light of what Barnabas told him, that likelihood
dimmed. No, for the first time since making Miss Covington's acquaintance, a different picture of the young woman
emerged, and it appealed to him.

Chapter 4

Colton heaved a satisfied sigh as he finished loading the bulging burlap sacks into the wagon. He planned to set out for Juniper Springs right after breakfast. The sale of the fine wool meant he could replenish their supplies, and he tucked his list into his hip pocket. He looked forward to drinking real coffee instead of chicory, and although Barnabas would never ask, Colton planned to bring home some peppermint sticks for his friend's sweet tooth.

Colton climbed aboard and clucked to the team. Barnabas worked at repairing the corral gate next to the barn and waved as Colton rounded the curve in the road. Colton always advised Barnabas to stick close to the barn whenever Colton had to be away. Did it mean he lacked faith, or was it simply prudent? Colton pursed his lips. Nothing wrong with being cautious.

The late April morning treated his senses with the fragrance of spring grass and dogwood. A hint of honeysuckle lingered in the air. Jingling harnesses and the clopping of hooves blended with the song of a mockingbird. The serenade put a smile on Colton's face.

Within the hour, Colton pulled the team to a halt in front of the Feed and Seed. Sloan Talbot stood out front with a record book, counting sacks of grain.

"Mornin', Sloan."

Talbot shaded his eyes and squinted. "Hey Colton." He peered into the back of the wagon. "You got somethin' for me?"

"We finished our shearing a day early." Colton set the brake and tied off the reins. "Sure am glad, too." He climbed down over the wheel.

Sloan glanced over the load. "What have you got there, about sixteen sacks?"

"Eighteen. The two bags tied with red cording are lambs wool." Colton nudged his hat farther back with his thumb. "Are the prices you quoted me last month still holding?"

"Far as I know." Sloan gestured toward the open door. "Bring 'em over here, and I'll start weighing them."

Colton hauled the sacks to the scale and watched as Sloan balanced each load with counterweights and tallied them up.

"Say, what do you think about Covington running for governor?"

Colton hoped he'd be able to take care of his business, pick up his supplies, and head home without having to engage in any debates about Shelby Covington. "He's not my first choice."

"You don't say? Why not?" Sloan appeared genuinely surprised that Colton wasn't a supporter of the local candidate.

"I don't feel he has the best interests of the small farmers at heart, and I suspect he'd lead us into secession." Colton dusted off his hat.

Sloan flapped one hand at Colton. "That ain't going to happen, because that Lincoln fellow can't win the presidential election." The man pointed toward the sky, as if testifying to gospel truth. "You mark my words. Either Breckenridge or Douglas is going to win the presidency, and all this talk of secession will fade away. Won't be no need with one of them running things in Washington." Sloan stopped short. "That's right, I forgot. You're one of those fellows who's speaking out against secession. Don't understand why you wouldn't want to preserve Georgia's right to choose the way of life we want to follow."

Colton drew in a slow breath. Sloan Talbot wasn't the first man with whom he'd disagreed over the issue of slavery. "But I do believe in preserving the right to choose. I believe all men should have that freedom." He paused, letting his words settle with the full impact of their meaning. "It's morally wrong for one man to own another."

Sloan smirked. "What are you talkin' about? You got yourself a slave out there at your place. You wouldn't be able to get all your work done without that boy of yours."

The words hung on the tip of Colton's tongue. Barnabas wasn't a slave any longer. He worked for Colton because that's what he chose, not because he was forced. Barnabas gave Colton an honest day's work and took pride in what he did, the way man was made to do. Yes, Barnabas was free, but telling Sloan would be like spitting into the wind.

Sloan smiled like a bird-fed cat and appeared to think he'd won the argument. Changing Sloan's mind was unlikely, but Colton had to try.

"I believe Abraham Lincoln is going to be our next president. Georgia's current governor, Joseph Brown, is indecisive. He's not taken a position one way or the other on

these issues. Shelby Covington thinks secession will preserve states' rights, but all it will preserve is big landowners' right to own slaves. If he's elected and alienates those
businesses in the north who purchase the goods produced
by Southerners, it will break the backs of the small farmers.

"But the ones who will suffer most of all are those people who are bought and sold at the slave markets and live in
bondage, forced to work like animals. Some live in worse
conditions than the animals. I can't vote for a man who
endorses slavery."

Sloan clamped his mouth closed. His lips thinned out
and curved downward at the corners. He closed his tally
book and tucked it under his arm. "You know, Colton, I
just remembered. I got a notice the other day from the
mills in New Jersey and Massachusetts that the price of
wool dropped. Ain't going to be able to pay you the price
I quoted last month." He stuck one thumb in his belt and
straightened his shoulders.

Colton stared at Sloan, a man he considered a friend. Or
he had at one time. A spark of anger ignited in his belly,
but he doused it. Going toe-to-toe with Sloan on the sidewalk wouldn't raise the price of wool, nor would it change
Sloan's thinking. "What is the going rate now?"

Sloan quoted a price per pound that equated to approximately half what Colton expected. Before he had a chance
to digest the bad news, Sloan tossed the record book down
on the boardwalk and spoke again. "Owen Dinsmore at the
freight depot tells me shipping rates are going up. He said it
costs twice as much to ship freight as it did last month. Must
be all those ugly rumors about Lincoln getting elected."
Sloan finished his declaration with a sneer.

Colton shook his head. "Would you mind showing me
that notice you received from the mills?"

Sloan lifted his shoulders and held out his hand, fingers

splayed. "My desk is so messy. It'd probably take me all day to find it."

"That's all right." Colton kept his tone even. "While you search for it, I'll go by the freight office and confirm that shipping price with Owen." He slid his gaze sideways at the stacked burlap sacks. "In the meantime, I'll just take my wool and load it back on the wagon so nobody makes a mistake and accidentally spills coal oil on it, or something like that."

He began hefting the packed wool into the back of the wagon, indignation swelling in his chest.

"There ain't no need for you to do that, Colton." As Colton expected, a thread of desperation rang in Sloan's voice at the prospect of losing his agent's commission.

Colton continued loading. It wasn't hard to figure out Sloan intended to get full price for the wool when he sold it to the Northern mills.

"Where else you going to take your goods? I'm the only agent in town who buys wool."

Colton didn't miss a beat. "You're not the only agent in north Georgia. The agents in Gainesville have always paid about three cents a pound more than you do. It'll take me a couple of days to get there and back, but the money will make the trip worthwhile. If Harry Jeffers in Gainesville tries to tell me the price of wool has dropped to half of its former price, I'll take it to Athens." He thumped a sack into the wagon and paused to shoot a pointed stare at Sloan. "I'm not giving my wool away."

Colton brushed past Sloan to pick up another sack. He hoped the apprehension over leaving Barnabas alone for a few days didn't show on his face as he continued to re-load the wagon. He lifted another sack and slung it to his shoulder. Before he could step off the boardwalk, Sloan caught his arm.

"Look, Colton. There's no need for this." He jerked his thumb toward the doorway leading to his office. "I don't think I can find that notice, and maybe I was mistaken about what it said. You know my memory ain't what it used to be." He took the sack from Colton's arms and tossed it back onto the boardwalk. "We'll just write up the deal for the same price as before and call it square. That all right with you?"

Colton leveled a stony gaze at Sloan. "That's always been all right with me. But know this. I won't continue to do business with a man who treats me unfairly because of a difference of opinion."

Without another word, Sloan picked up the record book and began tallying the weights he'd written down. A few moments later, he showed Colton the totals.

Colton gave a nod and a grunt. "That's a fair price. I'll just finish loading these sacks while you get my money."

Confusion etched deep wavy furrows across Sloan's forehead. "Where're you taking them?"

Colton lifted his eyebrows. "I just want to make sure they arrive at the freight depot safely. I'll be back in a half hour with the shipping invoice."

Sloan's face reddened and he curled his hands into fists at his sides, but he turned on his heel and stomped into the office.

Colton finished loading the sacks and turned the wagon around. Relief washed through him. Leaving Barnabas alone at the farm for days at a time, even with Free there to bark a warning, filled him with trepidation. After dropping off the wool at the freight depot, Colton confirmed his suspicions. Owen Dinsmore quoted him the same shipping rates as always.

Colton's rumbling stomach reminded him it was nearly

lunchtime. He pulled up at the hitching rail outside the mercantile and climbed three steps up to the boardwalk.

Clyde Sawyer greeted him as he entered. "Howdy, Colton. How's things out at your place?"

"Just fine, Clyde. How's Betsy?"

A wide smile filled Clyde's face, and his gray whiskers wiggled the way they always did when he spoke about his wife. "You know my Sweet Pea. She knows everything that goes on in Juniper Springs and doesn't mind talking about it. Jack McCaffey at the *Sentinel* told me the other day Betsy's going to put him out of business."

Colton grinned. "You better not let Betsy hear you say that."

"Did I hear my name?" The curtains dividing the storeroom from the front of the mercantile parted and a grayhaired woman with snapping green eyes stepped out. "Clyde, are you telling tales again?"

"Aw, Sweet Pea, you know I'd never do that." Clyde winked at Colton and lowered his voice to a conspiratorial whisper. "After you've been married for as long as me and my Sweet Pea, you learn to just let them have their way."

"I heard that." Betsy narrowed her eyes and batted her hand at her husband. "Now what can we do for you today, Colton?"

Colton pulled his list from his hip pocket and handed it to Betsy. "I have some empty crates in the wagon. Thought I'd go grab a bite to eat over at Maybelle's and pick up the supplies afterwhile."

Betsy sent Colton a warm smile. "That'll be fine. Clyde honey, go and get the crates out of Colton's wagon."

"Yes, Sweet Pea." Clyde's placating tone brought an immediate hissing sigh from his wife, but before she could retort, he pecked her on the cheek.

Colton guffawed. The couple pretended to fight like a

pair of alley cats at times, but their affection for each other was always evident. He backed up in mock wariness.

"Think I'll just go on to Maybelle's before the fur starts flying in here." He grinned at Clyde and exited.

He greeted a few folks on the boardwalk as he strode past the cabinetmaker and hotel. A small crowd gathered down the street near the newspaper office. As Colton approached, a man held up the latest edition of the *Sentinel*. Splashed across the front page, the headline read Covington Runs for Governor.

Auralie stepped out the door of the newspaper office having dropped off the note to the editor as her father had directed. She picked up her flowing lavender skirts to keep from dragging the hem in the dusty red clay as she and Mammy made their way across the street to Frances Hyatt's dressmaker shop for her fitting.

A small crowd congregated on the side of the street nearest the newspaper office. As she and Mammy stepped around them, Auralie heard one man declare, "Joseph Brown is bad enough, but Covington would make a worse governor than Brown, if that's possible."

She slowed her steps and listened to the derogatory remarks being made about her father.

"All Covington is interested in is putting more money in his own pocket."

"Speaking of money, did you read the part of that article about the Boldens? That entire clan is backing Covington."

"Thick as thieves, they are."

"What do you think, Colton?"

Auralie froze in her tracks. The very man whose image invaded her dreams stood among these people who had nothing but negative things to say about her father. She peered through the crowd and caught a glimpse of his profile, and her heart hiccupped.

"I believe we must examine our own conscience to determine whether or not a man like Shelby Covington is the best choice for governor. It's the responsibility of every man who casts a vote to seek God's guidance and not be swayed by unethical granting of political favors."

Auralie couldn't tear her eyes away from Colton. Deep in her heart, she couldn't deny what he said was true. When he finished speaking he turned, and for a fleeting moment their gazes collided. She tried to read his expression when he caught sight of her. His eyes softened into an apologetic grimace, but she doubted he regretted saying what he did. Only that she'd heard him say it. He lifted his hand and started to speak, but she spun around.

Deciding to forego the dress fitting, she snagged Mammy's arm and hurried toward the carriage, barely waiting long enough for their driver to open the door and hand her up to the seat.

"What is it, honey girl? What dem folks say what's got you all upset?"

Auralie sat in silence for a full minute clutching Mammy's hand. When she trusted her voice to speak without breaking, she replied in a voice so hushed, Mammy had to lean close.

"I don't think it's what they said so much as it is that I fear they are right. Father has always preached to me about the Covington name and how respected it is, but how can he force his own daughter into a marriage just so it will benefit him politically? Where is the respect in that?" Tears threatened and she pressed her eyes closed.

"You been prayin' on it like I tol' you?"

Auralie shook her head. "Sometimes I still feel like God

is so far off, so big and mighty and powerful. How could He care about someone like me?"

"Mmm-hmm." Mammy wrapped Auralie in her arms and hummed while rocking back and forth. "Oh honey girl, jes' you look at me. I ain't nuthin' but an ol' slave woman, and He care 'bout me."

Auralie straightened. "But how do you know?"

Pure bliss and adoration filled Mammy's face. "'Cause I done talked to Him jus' dis mornin'."

When the carriage finally turned into the long, winding drive that led to the main house, another carriage approached from the opposite direction heading toward the road. Auralie stared. The fine, ornate gray carriage drawn by a pair of perfectly matched black horses looked vaguely familiar. As the two carriages passed, Auralie's stomach clenched. She'd seen that carriage before. It belonged to Thaddeus Bolden, Perry's father.

She twisted in her seat trying to see the occupants, but the interior of the carriage was too shadowed. A shudder began in the pit of her stomach and traveled up her spine. Had Perry returned? Was he here? With trembling hands, she gripped the seat, wishing she could fly away like the dove in the psalm.

Chapter 5

Colton bent his back and swung the hoe at the weeds growing between the rows of knee-high corn, wishing he could rid himself of worries as easily as he hacked away the unwanted undergrowth. Rumblings about the upcoming elections and rumors of secession continued to spin out of control, and every time Colton went into town—even to church—the topic of discussion was as predictable as the sunrise. He carried on a running conversation with God, bringing the burdens of his heart to the throne, but it seemed no sooner had he laid one worry down another sprang up.

"Kind of like weeds." Colton and the Lord shared a smile.

He straightened and twisted to stretch the kinks in his muscles. Putting a hand to his forehead to shade his eyes, he searched the next field for Barnabas. The man could work circles around Colton. Judging by Barnabas's position, he had already planted more than half of the second cornfield.

Across the footpath, Free patrolled the meadow where the sheep grazed. A soft breeze stirred the trees, and the sun warmed the earth to bring forth a bountiful crop. Colton couldn't ask for a more peaceful scene. But an unsettled feeling of impending danger lurked, taunting him like a schoolyard bully.

"Lord, I don't know why I keep looking over my shoulder, waiting for some unseen catastrophe, but it's like an ache that won't go away, no matter how much I rub it. Pastor Winslow used to be able to tell when a storm was coming, even when the sky was clear. That's the way I feel. There's a storm on the horizon that I can't prevent. All I can do is ask You to be with us and give us shelter from the storm. Forgive me for trying to carry burdens that aren't mine to carry or control. Only You, Lord, can control the winds and the storms, no matter what form they take."

Free's bark interrupted Colton's prayer. He looked beyond the meadow and past the second cornfield into the trees. To the south of the cornfields lay a small apple orchard. Colton's searching gaze swept across the fields and beyond the orchard, but couldn't see any intruders—of the two- or four-legged variety. In the distance, his neighbor's house perched between several tall pines, but Colton could see no one stirring around there either.

When the sun was high overhead, Barnabas came tramping up the slope, carrying his shirt in one hand, his canteen slung over his shoulder. Colton joined him, and they hiked back to the house to see what they could scrape together for lunch.

Colton pumped water into a bucket and raised handfuls to his face to rinse off the sweat and dirt. "You've made great progress on that second field." He shook the water from his hair.

"It be finished by sundown. I's holdin' out some seed fo' one more plantin', jus' 'nough fo' another acre." Barnabas gulped down a dipper of water and then poured a second dipper over his head. "Ahh."

Colton tossed him a towel and went inside the cabin to put their lunch together. Barnabas came to the open door and knocked on the doorframe before stepping inside. Despite Colton's repeated invitations, the former slave couldn't seem to leave behind his old habits of submission. "Come on in. Grab a jar of those peaches from the pantry. There's some coffee left from breakfast. Push the pot over the fire while I make some biscuit and bacon sandwiches."

Barnabas smacked his lips. "Real coffee. Don' wanna waste none o' that."

They settled at the table, and Colton asked the blessing on the food. As they dug in, Barnabas pushed a stray crumb into his mouth. "Seen some men pokin' around in the woods out pas' the orchard this mornin' while I's workin'."

Colton almost choked on the bite of biscuit in his mouth. "Slave catchers? What were they doing? I wondered what Free was barking at."

"Don' think dey's bounty hunters, didn't look like it. Dey seen me workin' but didn' pay much mind. Deys mo' interested in the trees, and they done some pointin' and lookin' 'round. One of 'em had some kind o' spyglass settin' up on three legs. He point it 'cross yo' land and look through it and write sumpin' on a paper."

Colton leaned back in his chair. "Surveyors maybe? But I can't imagine what they were looking at across my fields. Have you ever seen any of them before?"

Barnabas's hesitation in answering piqued Colton's concern.

"Meybe. One of 'em look familiar, like meybe I seen him long time ago." He took another bite of biscuit and rubbed his chin while he chewed, like he was turning something over in his mind. "Don' wanna say fo' sho'. I might be wrong."

Colton let him think on it while they ate in silence for a couple of minutes. After they finished off the peaches, Colton poured the last of the coffee into their tin cups. "Well, do you think you know who the man was that you saw?"

Barnabas blew on his coffee and took a noisy slurp. "Could be. Seem like the one fella put me in mind o' Massah Covington's boy."

"Shelby Covington's son?"

"Mm hm. Massah Dale Covington. I ain't seen him in a mighty long time, but sho' did look like him."

"That's peculiar—if it was him. What would Dale Covington be doing tramping around in the woods next to my land?"

Auralie tapped on the door of her mother's sitting room and cocked her head to listen for Phoebe Covington's soft response. The woman never raised her voice, and most times spoke so softly one had to strain to hear her.

Auralie cracked the door open. "Mother? May I come in?"

"Come in, Auralie."

Mother sat on her ivory satin brocade chaise with flowing skirts primly arranged around her ankles. Her impeccably coiffed ash blond hair crowned her delicate features, and a leather-bound volume with gold filigree edging the corners graced her soft hands. One might think she was posing to have her portrait painted.

"Mother, I need to ask you something."

A hint of disapproval flickered across her mother's porcelain complexion, dipping her eyebrows and accentuating the tiny lines across her forehead—lines she never admitted existed.

"Auralie. You are no longer a child, and therefore should have learned long ago how a refined lady enters a room." She wafted the air with one hand in a graceful gesture. "Proper etiquette dictates we step softly, courteously greet those present, and engage in polite conversation."

Auralie stifled a sigh. She loved her mother but grieved the distance between them, even when they were in the same room. Phoebe Covington embodied the epitome of everything Auralie resented but dared not express. "I apologize, Mother. How are you this morning?"

"I'm quite well, thank you. And you?" Mother gave a slight nod, as if prompting Auralie to respond in kind.

Eager to dispense with the formalities, Auralie answered with the replies she'd been trained to give. For a fleeting moment she envied the daughters who could share trivial things with their mothers, like the new dresses she'd ordered from Frances Hyatt.

"Please sit down." Mother gestured to a nearby chair, also upholstered in ivory brocade. "Shall I ring for tea?"

"No thank you." Auralie took her seat. The request she came to make fidgeted within her for expression. "It's a lovely morning."

Her mother sent her gaze to the window. "Yes it is. Perhaps this afternoon I shall walk in the garden before tea."

"I'm sure the outing will be quite pleasant."

"Auralie, will you please refrain from doing that."

Auralie blinked and dropped her guarded bearing. "Doing what?"

Exasperation edged her mother's carefully controlled tone. "A proper lady does not show nervousness by twisting her ring."

Auralie glanced down at her hands and pulled her fingers away from the sapphire ring, gently interlacing them instead. "Mother, I've received a message this morning from Cousin Belle."

"And what does your cousin have to say?"

Auralie willed her hands to be still. "As you know, her husband, Lloyd, is away in Atlanta on business."

"I was not aware of that."

"Yes, an architectural firm in Atlanta has requested several drawings from him for a project. It seems they admire his work and have retained him for a rather prestigious undertaking." She paused to gauge her mother's reaction, but could not detect any emotion one way or the other on the woman's face. "It will require that he be away from home for several weeks, and Belle hasn't being feeling well. She has asked that I come and stay with her for a while, until Lloyd returns home."

Her mother pressed a lace handkerchief to her lips. "I see. Have you spoken with your father about this?"

"No." Her fingers encircled the ring again. "I was hoping you could ask him for me."

For the first time since Auralie entered the room, her mother allowed her poised demeanor to slip, and Auralie glimpsed apprehension.

"You must send word to your father that you wish to speak with him and request that he inform you what time would be convenient." Her mother's reply wasn't what Auralie wanted to hear. She'd hoped for an advocate in coaxing her father to give his permission, but now she must enter the lion's den alone.

Auralie drew in a silent breath and held it, awaiting her father's response to Cousin Belle's request. Stepping inside his study felt akin to approaching a king's throne room, and Auralie fought the urge to run. She sat on the fine leather chair in front of the massive polished desk and locked her crossed ankles under her skirt in an attempt to imitate her mother's perfect posture.

Her father's scowl made her shrink into the chair despite her best efforts to emulate her mother's grace. He tossed the folded note across the desk, and his voice boomed within the walnut walls of the stately room.

"Do I need to remind you we are awaiting Perry Bolden's return, which could be any time." He picked up a brandy snifter and swirled the amber liquid in the glass before taking a sip. Auralie hated the effect the drink had on her father and usually hid herself away in her room whenever he indulged—especially so early in the day.

"Yes sir, I'm aware of that. The new gowns I commissioned are ready, the invitations have been written and are waiting to be sent, and Cook is planning the menu for the—" The word strangled in her throat. She covered her mouth with her fingertips and coughed. "Excuse me. The menu for the…engagement party."

"Then you know that your presence is required here." Father stood and paced behind his desk. "Thaddeus Bolden was here last week to finalize some…details. He said the last letter he received from his son indicated Perry would set sail from England on April twenty-fifth."

"But that was just a week ago. A trans-Atlantic voyage takes—"

"I'm well aware of how long it takes." He tossed down the remainder of his brandy and poured himself another.

Auralie's pulse pounded in her ears and her throat tightened. Her fingers shook as she twisted the ring and waited for her father to continue the tirade she knew was imminent.

As she expected, his voice gained volume as he repeated his expectations that she make herself available to the Boldens and reminded her how important this union would be to his political aspirations. He slammed the brandy glass down on his desk, sending shards of glass sailing in multiple directions. An involuntary flinch rippled over her. She instinctively yanked up her hands in a defensive posture and drew back.

"When are you going to learn to maintain an attitude of dignity instead of sitting there simpering like an empty-headed fool? Perry Bolden wants a woman of elegance and composure by his side, not one that quavers at the sound of a man's voice."

Auralie's stomach twisted into a knot, and her trembling hands grew clammy. Without warning, the image of Colton Danfield manifested in her mind along with a fleeting thought that she doubted he was the type of man to intimidate a woman. She had no basis for her belief, other than the warmth of his dark eyes and the quiet way he'd recommended the people around him seek God's wisdom in casting their vote. She blinked the image away. Her father towered before her like an overlord awaiting her response.

She raised her chin and adjusted her posture. Her voice must sound perfectly modulated and controlled, ringing with the grace her father demanded. And it was.

"Of course, Father. I'm merely requesting your permission to visit with Cousin Belle for a time. She lives less than an hour away. I could return home immediately should we receive word that Perry has arrived."

Father planted both hands on the desk and leaned forward, leveling a sinister glare at her. "You'd better hope to Saint Peter you'll return home immediately."

A spark of hope ignited in her middle. Did that mean he was letting her go?

Father bellowed for one of the house slaves to bring him another glass then resumed his barking about "her duty." With one final admonition, laced with a threat about her not embarrassing him, he waved his hand in dismissal.

She struggled to control her feet to refrain from taking wing as she exited the study. The moment the door was closed, she fairly flew up the grand, curving staircase to find Mammy. When Auralie burst into her bedroom, Mammy startled, jerking her head away from her task of putting freshly laundered clothes in Auralie's bureau.

"Mercy, chile. Where you goin' in such a hurry?"

A silly grin stretched her lips, and she grasped Mammy's hands. "I'm going to visit Cousin Belle. And you're coming with me."

"Massah Covington say yes? Dat be a s'prise to me."

Giddiness crept up Auralie's throat and emerged as a giggle. "He didn't say no. He just said I have to return immediately if we get word that Perry Bolden has arrived."

A smile played around Mammy's lips. "I send one of the menservants to bring yo' trunk down. When we leavin'?"

"As soon as possible." She sat down at the small secretary and pulled out her stationery box and pot of ink. "It will only take a minute to write this note to Cousin Belle. Can you please call Reuben to take it over to her? Then I'll help you pack."

"Give my heart joy to see you this happy, honey girl. You deserve dis kind o' happiness."

She scribbled the note and blew on the ink to hasten its drying while Mammy went to find the coachman to transport the note to Belle. Auralie sat back and closed her eyes. Imagine having the freedom to come and go as she pleased indefinitely. Realization pinched her stomach. Her happiness was short-lived. Looming in her future like a vulture over a dead animal was her forthcoming marriage to Perry and a lifetime of living just like her mother.

Chapter 6

Auralie sipped the glass of lemonade Belle handed her and leaned back against the porch swing. Regardless of how long or short her visit with her cousin, she intended to enjoy every minute, like a prisoner being handed a commuted sentence.

Squirrels argued in a nearby oak tree, and a pair of wrens flitted back and forth to their nest where three scrawny heads raised up with beaks wide open every time one of the parents landed on the adjacent branch. A lazy white cat stretched out at the opposite end of the porch.

"Aren't you afraid the cat will get to the baby birds?"

Belle laughed, a delightful tinkling sound, and shook her head. "No. Frank is too old and fat to be a danger to anything other than the scraps we feed him. I've never seen a cat sleep as much as he does." She picked up a sugar cookie and nibbled on the golden edge. "Have you decided how long you can stay?"

Auralie sighed. "If it was up to me, I'd stay indefinitely—at least until Lloyd comes back. But Father says I must return home the moment we receive word that Perry Bolden is back."

Belle pooched her bottom lip out in a feigned pout. "I still can't believe that you didn't tell me you were engaged. I thought I was your favorite cousin."

Auralie blew out a stiff breath. "You *are* my favorite cousin, but—" She lowered her voice. "This engagement isn't anything I wanted to celebrate."

"What?" Belle's eyes widened and she set her lemonade down. "What do you mean?"

"Belle, I haven't laid eyes on Perry Bolden since you and I were in pigtails. Thaddeus Bolden and Father arranged this marriage four years ago. Father announced it to me and Mother on my sixteenth birthday, as if it were a grand birthday gift, and I'm expected to go along with it."

Her cousin's round blue eyes glistened. "Oh Auralie, how awful. I can't even imagine joining myself in marriage to a man I didn't love. Didn't Aunt Phoebe object?"

Auralie shrugged. "If she did, she certainly didn't tell me. You know Mother. She wouldn't dream of going against anything Father says, or even letting him think she has an opinion." She rose and walked to the railing where Belle's roses were just beginning to bloom. "All during our childhood, we never stopped to consider those people who don't have a choice about their lives. They do as they're told and are completely subservient to their owners."

Belle cocked her head. "Are you talking about the slaves? What do they have to do with you marrying Perry Bolden?"

"Don't you see? We're alike." Auralie returned to sit sideways facing Belle on the swing. "Once I'm married to Perry, I'll be living in just as much bondage as any of the slaves."

Defensiveness threaded Belle's voice. "You say *bondage* like all slaves are treated cruelly."

"You must admit that some are, even if ours are not. Mammy is dearer to me than my own parents." She gestured toward the back end of the porch. Beyond the railing and on the opposite side of the vegetable garden, the summer kitchen sat separated from the main house. Within its walls, Mammy helped Belle's servants. "You grew up with Sam and Maizie in your home, and when you married Lloyd, your father gave them to you. But think about it. Even though they have a good home here and you treat them well, they don't have a choice about their lives, and neither do I."

Belle's expression grew perplexed. "I think I see your point, but surely being married to Perry can't be equated to being a slave. His family is wealthy. You'll have a beautiful home, the finest clothes, servants to do your bidding—you'll never want for anything."

"Except the thing I crave the most—a man who loves me. A man for me to love in return."

"There's nothing you can do?"

Auralie shook her head. "Nothing, short of sneaking out my window in the middle of the night and running away. Where could I go that Father couldn't follow and find me?"

They sat in silence for a while, and Auralie let the gentle rocking of the swing soothe her frazzled nerves. Lloyd and Belle's house was small compared to the sprawling manor house in which she lived. The house she'd been told Perry was having built was even grander. But Belle's house felt much more like a home. Belle didn't have fifteen bedrooms, a lavish ballroom, or an elegant study. There was no immense dining room big enough to seat a dinner party of forty. The gardens surrounding the place were not ostentatious. But there was something the Covington plantation house lacked. Genuine, heartfelt love.

Belle stood and stretched. "I think Maizie is making roast chicken for dinner. I hope that's all right. You're probably used to much fancier meals."

"Roast chicken sounds marvelous." She joined her cousin and they went back into the house. A large bookcase filled almost an entire wall on one end of the spacious front parlor, and Belle's curio cabinet sat in the corner displaying china doll figurines that she'd collected since she was a girl.

"I remember some of these." Auralie picked up one with golden hair swirled up like a crown and wearing a stunning ball gown with flowers around the edge and a daring neckline. "This one was always my favorite. Remember we used to dream about dressing up in beautiful gowns and waltzing all evening with dashing young gentlemen lined up waiting their turn?" She returned the figurine to its shelf. "Isn't it ironic how the things we dreamed of and wished for as young girls are now the very things I dread?" She ran her fingers over several of the dolls.

Belle took her hand. "Is it the marriage you dread?"

Hearing Belle voice the question helped Auralie put it into perspective. "It's more than just the marriage. I'm… restless, and frustrated at the role I'm expected to fill. I wish I could have goals and ambitions, but I feel like one of these china dolls—nice to look at, perhaps, but serving no purpose."

"Oh Auralie, you have a purpose. You're a sweet person, kindhearted and sensitive to the feelings of others."

She turned to face her cousin. "But I have nothing to occupy my time and my hands, nothing I can do to make a difference in someone's life. All that is expected of a well-bred, Southern lady is to marry well." She grasped Belle's hand and urgency filled her voice. "I want more than that, but I don't know what." She shook her head. "I know what I *don't* want, but I don't know what I *do* want."

Belle slipped her arms around Auralie and hugged her close. "Then we shall pray for God to show you."

"Belle, are you ever afraid of God?"

"Goodness, no!" Belle jerked her head back and looked Auralie in the eye. "Why would you be afraid of a God who loves you?"

Auralie bit her lip. She didn't want to be afraid of God, but she couldn't comprehend a Father who loved and cared for her like the Bible promised He did. She sighed deep within the recesses of her soul.

Auralie took the cup of weak tea Maizie handed her and smiled her thanks to the gray-haired black woman who clucked her tongue like a fretting hen.

"I stirred some honey in it. Miss Belle like her tea sweet. She need sumpin' on her stomach, and she didn't eat no breakfas'."

Before Auralie could turn to carry the tea upstairs to Belle, Maizie stopped her. "Miss Auralie, meybe she listen to you if you tell her go see the doctor."

Maizie's concern touched Auralie. She sounded just like Mammy. "I think I've convinced her to go. Could you please ask Sam to hitch the carriage?"

Maizie beamed. "Sam sho' be glad to do that. I'll go tell 'im right now."

Auralie climbed the staircase to Belle's room and found her cousin pale and blotting her face with a damp cloth.

"Are you feeling any better?"

"A little. This doesn't last all day. It comes and goes."

Auralie set the teacup down on the bedside table. "Maizie made you some tea. She said you needed to put something in your stomach."

A faint smile lifted Belle's lips. "That's Maizie's answer for every ailment. I probably just need a tonic or something."

"Sam is hitching up the carriage." Auralie covered Belle's hand with hers. "Are you sure you don't want me to go with you?"

"No, I'll be fine." Belle took a few sips of tea, rose from the bed, and patted her hair in place. "Besides, I need to stop by Pastor Shuford's house and speak with him about having someone take the children's Sunday school class— at least until I'm feeling better."

"All right." Auralie hugged her cousin. "I think I'll explore your bookshelves while you're gone."

Belle picked up her parasol and they descended the stairs. "Help yourself. If you'd like to go for a walk, there are some lovely wildflowers in the meadow between our house and our neighbor."

Auralie watched Sam solicitously hand Belle up into the carriage and make sure she was comfortably seated before climbing up to the driver's seat and urging the horses forward. Auralie sighed as she watched them leave and whispered a prayer that whatever ailed her cousin could, indeed, be remedied with a simple tonic.

The last time she recalled having a day all to herself, she was a carefree child with no more concerns than plucking petals from daisies. Perhaps she'd take that walk later and see if she could find some daisies to grace their dinner table.

She found a volume of *Wuthering Heights* on the parlor bookshelf. Smiling, she carried it out to the shady side porch and curled up in a cushioned rocker. Emily Brontë's story and characters mesmerized her—the brooding Heathcliff and the beautiful and free-spirited Catherine—and she was surprised when Mammy poked her head out and asked if she wanted her lunch brought out.

"My goodness, I must have lost track of time." She tucked a piece of ribbon between the pages to mark her place and stood to stretch. "Just something light, Mammy. I'm not terribly hungry."

Mammy returned a few minutes later with a tray. "Maizie and me make chicken salad from that roast chicken las' night. She say she don' never throw away food dat's lef', and Miss Belle don' mind at all." She set the tray on the small wicker table beside the rocker. "Maizie's makin' a fresh pitcher o' lemonade. I tol' her it one o' yo' fav'rites."

The chicken salad was delicious and Auralie ate every bite. A warm breeze swayed the treetops and set the wild-flowers and grasses to dancing, inviting Auralie to join in the celebration of spring. She shaded her eyes and gazed out across the meadow to see if any daisies bloomed. Instead, she caught sight of two men working in a field beyond the boundary of Belle's place. One was a black man, bent over his task. The other arrested her attention. Even at a distance he looked familiar. She studied him for a minute, the way he moved, the angle at which he held his head.

"Colton Danfield."

Belle said she had neighbors but didn't mention the name. She observed the two men working side by side for a time. Peculiar…she'd gotten the impression from the way he spoke in town that he was against slavery, but the Negro man laboring beside him indicated differently.

Colton jerked his glance up when Free started barking. A woman walked toward them carrying a jug of some sort. Her wheat-colored hair peeked out from a wide-brimmed green bonnet. Even though the bonnet prevented him from seeing her face, his pulse picked up when she drew closer. It couldn't be…

"Freedom, hush up."

The dog quieted but remained on alert, watching the stranger approach.

Colton quickly buttoned his shirt and strode to meet the visitor. He ran his hands over his wind-tossed hair to push it into submission and brushed at his clothes in a vain attempt to rid himself of some of the dirt he'd attracted.

"Miss Covington." His voice sounded unnatural and forced. "This is a surprise."

Her smile rivaled the spring sunshine. "For me as well. I had no idea you were my cousin's neighbor."

"Lloyd Hancock is your cousin?"

"No, his wife, Belle. I'm visiting with her for a while."

"I see." He eyed the pitcher and cups in her hands.

"When I saw the two of you working so hard, I thought you might like something cool to drink." She held out the two cups. "I also felt I owed you an apology."

Colton took the cups and held them while she poured lemonade into them. "An apology? You've done nothing for which to apologize."

"Oh, but I did, Mr. Danfield. You started to speak to me in town the other day and I rudely turned and walked away from you."

Colton handed one of the cups to Barnabas, who lowered his eyes and gave a slight nod.

"Thank you kindly, miss."

Colton watched Barnabas take a long drink. Perhaps he'd been wrong about Auralie Covington. He turned and gave her an appreciative smile. "Thank you. This was very kind of you, but I fear it's I who owe you the apology. You heard me say some rather uncomplimentary things about your father—"

"Things that were true." She finished his sentence.

Colton blinked his surprise at her candor. "I'm still sorry you heard me say it. I'm afraid when one runs for political office he is vulnerable to public criticism from those who disagree with him."

"I'm not blaming you for disagreeing with my father. Truth be told, I disagree with him myself, but nobody asks a woman's opinion."

Yes, he could say with all confidence that he'd been completely wrong about this woman. "Well, thank you again for the lemonade."

She tipped her head to one side. "May I ask you a question?"

"Of course."

She began in a hesitant voice. "When I heard you speak in town, at the meeting in the café and again on the street, I got the impression you were against slavery."

Colton nodded. "Yes ma'am, I am."

Confusion wrinkled her brow, and she glanced over to Barnabas and back to Colton. "But—"

"Barnabas isn't my slave. He's my employee. I pay him a wage. Not a big wage, but certainly more than he ever got as a slave." He cast a quick look over his shoulder and caught Barnabas listening to every word. Colton turned back to Miss Covington. "I realize the law states that once a slave has been freed, it's the responsibility of the owner who freed him to ensure that he leave the state. However, Barnabas is also my friend and as such has chosen to remain and work with me. Just to make sure everything is done decently and in order, he made his mark on an indenture agreement, but it's merely a formality. If Barnabas wanted to leave here tomorrow, I'd make sure he had safe passage to wherever he wished to go."

Her eyes widened, not in shock but with enlightenment. Warmth flooded Colton as he watched her smile.

"Mammy is more than my friend. I can't describe how dear she is to me." Her smile faded. "But she's still a slave because she belongs to my father."

Colton nodded. An affinity grew between them. "God holds the times and seasons in His hand. I believe some changes are on the horizon, hopeful changes, but I fear the circumstances to achieve those changes might be tragic."

Chapter 7

Auralie stepped into the summer kitchen the next morning. Mouthwatering aromas of bacon, biscuits, and fresh coffee greeted her.

Mammy looked up from the fresh strawberries she was cleaning. "What you doin' downstairs so early, honey girl?"

Maizie glanced at her. "Miss Belle sick again, ain't she?" She and Mammy exchanged a meaningful look. "Why don' you go on up an' sit wi' her, and I'll bring up a tray of chamomile tea and dry toast."

Auralie twisted her ring. "I don't know if she'll be able to eat anything yet. She's quite ill." At the moment, food lost its appeal for her as well. "I'm worried about her."

A tiny smile poked a dimple in Mammy's cheek, and she patted Auralie's shoulder. "Don' you fret, honey girl. I 'spect the doctor know what the problem be. You go on up to her now. When she ready, she tell you her news."

News? That seemed a strange way to refer to one being

as sick as Belle, but Auralie didn't linger for an explanation. She picked up the hem of her dressing gown and hurried up the stairs.

Belle sat on the small balcony outside the French doors in her bedroom. "The fresh air seems to help. I couldn't abide that awful smell."

Awful smell? Auralie sniffed, thinking perhaps the wind had shifted and was coming from the direction of the stables, but the only thing she could smell was breakfast cooking. "Didn't Doctor Greenway give you any medicine?"

A weak smile wobbled across Belle's face. "No. As far as he knows there's no medicine that can fix me."

Auralie's heart turned over. "Oh Belle, I—"

"Sit down, cousin. I have something to tell you, and it's good news. The best news."

What a brave woman her cousin was, facing an illness the doctor declared incurable with a smile on her face. Auralie sat opposite her and reached to take her hands, determined to be strong for her cousin.

Belle's smile deepened. "Doctor Greenway says I'm expecting."

Expecting? "What are you exp— Oh! You're...you're..." She clapped both hands over her mouth.

Belle giggled. "I wanted to wait until Lloyd came home so he could be the first person I told, but under the circumstances, I don't think I could keep you in a state of worry any longer." She laughed again. "I think Maizie and Mammy already figured it out."

Auralie threw her arms around her cousin. "I couldn't be happier for you. I just hate it that you're sick."

Belle placed her hand over her stomach and took a couple of slow, deep breaths. "Yes, well, Doctor Greenway said that would pass in a few weeks. I hope he's right."

"Let me bring you a shawl if you're going to sit out

here on the balcony." Auralie found a shawl on a hook in Belle's wardrobe cabinet. She hurried back to the balcony and draped the wrap over her cousin's shoulders. "Did the doctor say when the baby might come?"

"Late autumn. At least by Thanksgiving." A crease carved a path between Belle's brows and tiny waves of alarm rippled through Auralie.

"Is there something else? Did the doctor say you were all right?"

"I'm fine." Belle patted Auralie's hand and sighed. "I picked up the mail while I was in town. There was a letter from Lloyd. He says he's being retained by the architectural firm in Atlanta."

"That's wonderful!" Auralie clapped her hands then caught the faraway look in Belle's eye. "Isn't it?"

"Yes. It will keep him in Atlanta longer than we planned, but he's worked very hard for this." She turned her head. "All this talk about secession and forming a state militia…"

Auralie sensed her cousin's concern. "Are you afraid Lloyd might join the Georgia Militia?"

A single tear made its way down Belle's cheek, heightening Auralie's concern. "The elections will be held in early November. If Mr. Lincoln is elected and Georgia secedes…" Her voice broke. "It makes me wonder if Lloyd will even be here for the birth of his child."

Everyone else in the house had gone to bed hours ago, but Auralie sat in the bedroom window seat watching a storm build toward the northwest, not unlike the tempest unfurling in her soul. Mammy and Belle had both encouraged her to pray, but uncertainty jerked her this way and that until she no longer knew how to pray. The realization startled her. What if she prayed wrong? What if this marriage to Perry *was* God's will? If she asked God to stop it, wouldn't He be angry with her? She lit a candle to chase her doubts into hiding.

Flashes illuminated the oak tree nearest the window in a ghoulish glow. Each rumble of thunder built on the last, as if in competition with each other. An unearthly yowl sent shivers up Auralie's spine, and the next flash of lightning revealed Belle's cat, Frank, crouched on a branch of the tree.

Auralie opened the window. "Frank, do you want to come in before this storm hits?"

As if understanding every word she said, Frank meowed, shinnied across the limb as close to the window as he could, and leaped gracefully to the windowsill. He preened for a moment then hopped down into the bedroom.

Auralie laughed. "Belle said you were too old and fat to climb trees. Won't she be surprised?"

Maow. Frank rubbed against her leg then proceeded to make himself at home on the foot of her bed. She rubbed his head and he purred in response, leaning into her touch.

"You can stay here tonight, old fellow, as long as it's storming. It'll be our secret."

Lightning flickered again, followed by a roll of thunder that seemed to rumble endlessly across the nearby mountains and echo in the valley beyond. The call of the storm drew her back to the window seat where she watched nature's wrath in fascination. Rain that had begun as a soft sprinkle now intensified. She closed the window and listened to it tapping on the glass like an evil thing demanding entrance. The similarity to the impending upheaval in her own life was too uncanny. She shuddered.

Forks of lightning sent jagged slashes across the sky. Bewildering emotions roiled within her in rhythm to each clap of thunder. Yesterday's visit to Colton Danfield's place left her feeling even more unsettled than her dread over Perry Bolden's return. Here she was, engaged to one of the richest young men in the state, from a very influential family. Yet she couldn't stop thinking about Colton Danfield—a man with dirt under his fingernails, who made his living by sweat and calluses. What did she have in common with him?

Learning the black man working on Colton's land was no longer a slave intrigued her. Curiosity picked at her to learn how the man's freedom came about. She'd heard accounts of men buying slaves only to set them free and wondered if that's what Colton had done. Speculation of him doing such a thing didn't seem far-fetched at all. In fact, the more she learned about this man, the more she wanted to know.

Thunder boomed and shook the house like a definition of her father's intimidating roar. A tremble rattled through her, imagining his response if he could read her thoughts. The storm raging outside her window was nothing compared with the maelstrom that would hail down around her if she defied Shelby Covington.

The booming thunder awakened Colton, and he rose from his bed. Crossing the cabin to the front door, he peered out through the sheets of rain to the barn, its form outlined by flares of lightning. Everything seemed in order. The sheep were safely tucked into the barn with Free, and his presence kept them calm despite the storm.

He returned to his bed and stared up at the ceiling, the interesting analogy drawing lines of perspective in his mind. Unsettled times, debate over political opinions, and the outcome of elections drew frightening pictures of possible consequences. But if one remembered the Shepherd who never slept—the One who always guarded and sheltered His children from the storms of life the way Free guarded and calmed the sheep—he could rest in the Shepherd's promise. A small smile lifted the corners of Colton's lips.

There was one thought, however, that kept slumber at bay. The image of Auralie Covington stepped into his mind. The memory of her walking through the meadow grass, the wind catching her hair and tugging it from the confines of her bonnet, lingered in Colton's subconscious like a drop of honey on his tongue. The sweetness remained long after the source was gone.

Colton listened to the storm retreating in the distance, grateful for the rain that nourished the earth. Rain to a farmer should be a soothing lullaby, but sleep slipped into some elusive hiding place. He needed his rest to energize him for the day's work ahead. He closed his eyes. Surely if he lay very still, slumber would overtake him.

It didn't.

How was he supposed to sleep when a woman like Auralie graced his thoughts? He rose to sit on the side of his bed, wondering if the storm had awakened Barnabas in the lean-to. Perhaps, but the man likely rolled over and went back to snoring. Colton stood and groped his way in the darkness to the east-facing window. No streaks of dawn painted the sky yet.

He felt his way to the table and lit the oil lamp. The soft glow danced across the room. He nudged the wick a little higher and the light grew. One of his mother's favorite scriptures eased into his memory.

"But if we walk in the light, as He is in the light, we have fellowship one with another, and the blood of Jesus Christ His Son cleanseth us from all sin."

"Lord, keep reminding me if I stay close to Your light, I'll always be able to see where I'm going."

He made his way to the small kitchen and shoved a few pieces of stove wood into the banked coals. While the stove heated, he measured ground coffee beans into the pot and ladled water over them. If sleep refused to be his companion, he could always count on the Lord and a fresh cup of coffee.

He pushed the pot over the hottest part of the stove and crossed the room to stand at the window. Distant lightning flickered within the clouds, like summer fireflies at dusk playing tag in and out of the field grasses. He tried to fix his eyes on the spot where he thought the next glimmer would be, only to have it blink in a different direction. Gratitude filled him as the scripture continued to roll through his mind. He didn't have to chase God's light, wondering where it might next appear. He could put his trust in the Lord's presence, knowing it was always constant.

The bracing aroma of coffee called to him, and he answered the beckoning invitation to fill a cup. He pulled out a chair and settled at the table where he'd left his Bible last night.

He opened the Book to Isaiah seeking encouragement for his heart. He soaked up the words, letting them bathe him in the comforting presence of the One who inspired their writing. He drained one cup of coffee and poured another, eager to return to the precious fellowship he found between the pages of God's Word. By the time he finished his second cup, pale light gilded the sky out the east window.

The latch on the back door rattled, and Barnabas knocked on the doorframe. "Mistah Colton? You got the coffeepot on already?"

"Come in, Barnabas. The Lord and I were having a talk."

Barnabas grinned. "I's finished with the barn chores. Me 'n' Free took the sheeps out to the pasture. Looks like it rained durin' the night."

Colton smirked. "You could say that." He gestured toward the stove. "Help yourself to the coffee."

Barnabas leaned and stared closely at Colton. "You don'

look like you slep' at all. Meybe I best make breakfas' so's it be fit to eat."

The offer coaxed a smile from Colton. "Fine with me."

"My mama's co'n cakes." Barnabas smacked his lips. "Wit' sorghum syrup." He pulled a cloth sack from the shelf and held it up. "Mistah Colton, this be co'nmeal?"

Colton turned up the flame flickering in the lamp. "No, that's grits. The other one is cornmeal."

Within minutes, corn cakes sizzled on the cast-iron griddle adding their fragrance to the air.

"There be four or five ewe sheeps that still ain't birthed their young'uns."

Colton grunted in response.

"I think two of 'em is carryin' twins."

"Maybe."

"Mistah Colton, you feelin' all right?"

"Fine. Just tired."

With a deft flip of his wrist, Barnabas turned the corn cakes. "Sump'in mo' than that botherin' you." A knowing twinkle glittered in his eyes.

If there was ever another soul on this earth besides his parents and Pastor Winslow that Colton knew he could trust, it was Barnabas. He stood and walked to the stove, poured himself another cup of coffee, and wandered back to the table. How did a man blurt out—even to a trusted friend—that he couldn't get a woman off his mind?

"Those corn cakes smell good."

Barnabas scooped the crispy cakes onto two plates, placing one in front of Colton. They bowed their heads, and Barnabas began to speak to God.

"Lawd, I thankin' You for this new day and the way You take care o' us. An' Lawd, please bless my frien', Mistah Colton. He be troubled this mornin', but I 'spect You already know 'bout dat. Now I ask You to be blessin' this here food, Lawd. It ain't as good as my mama made, but if You blessin' it, I be mighty thankful. In the name o' Your precious Son, sweet Jesus." When Barnabas raised his head, that same twinkle appeared in his eye, but Colton wasn't in the mood for teasing.

"Pass the syrup."

Barnabas pushed the syrup jug across the table, a twitch jiggling one corner of his mouth. "Womens sho' is puzzlin', ain't they?"

Colton sucked in a deep breath and blew it out. The man's ability to read his thoughts was downright uncanny. "I'm beginning to find that out." He stabbed a bite of corn cake and shoveled it into his mouth. He chewed thoughtfully for a minute and pointed his fork at Barnabas. "You know what bothers me?"

"Mmm-hmm, she be a pretty woman an' you don' know what to say to her."

An exasperated scowl twisted Colton's lips. "Besides that." He poked another forkful of corn cake into his mouth. "You lived on the Covington Plantation for over fifteen years, yet she acted like she didn't know you."

Barnabas shrugged. "No reason fo' her to know me. I was a field slave. All dem times she come down to Slave Row, she jus' be with the chilluns and some o' the mamas. She never did talk much to us workers, 'cause the overseer always around. I know who she be, but she never seen me."

"Hm." Colton mulled over Barnabas's reasoning. "Makes sense, I suppose." Colton polished off his breakfast and gulped the last of his coffee. He started to clear the table, but Barnabas stopped him.

"I take care o' the dishes, Mistah Colton. It be the Lawd's day. You gots to get ready fo' church."

Colton nodded, and for the hundredth time, wished Barnabas could come to church with him.

Chapter 8

Colton hated that Barnabas couldn't accompany him to the church in Juniper Springs. Leaving a man of Barnabas's faith behind to worship alone felt so wrong. There was no doubt in his mind his friend would spend time worshipping the God he loved, whether it took place in the barn, out in the meadow with Free and the sheep, or between the rows of growing corn. Barnabas never let a day go by without thanking God for His blessings. The way Barnabas found joy in the little things most people took for granted taught Colton that none of God's blessings were insignificant.

Colton finished shaving and dressing and pulled Pastor Winslow's black worsted wool coat from its hook. Slipping his arms into the sleeves, his memory echoed with the words of admonishment from the white-haired gentleman.

"Son, don't ever forsake the assembling with other believers on the Lord's Day."

Wearing the old preacher's coat to worship seemed like the man accompanied him. The thought made Colton smile.

Barnabas had Jasper saddled and ready when Colton stepped out the door. He mounted up and noticed his saddle had been freshly soaped and polished. Like he always did, Colton asked if Barnabas had his papers with him, and his friend responded by patting his shirt pocket. The practice had become a ritual.

Puddles dotted the road to town, and Colton carefully guided the horse around them so he wouldn't arrive at church mud-spattered. He drew in a deep breath of rain-washed air and remembered to thank God for providing the precipitation.

"And God, please watch over Barnabas while I'm gone. Keep him safe and let him find joy in his time of worship this morning."

Jasper's rocking chair gait made for an easy ride. Lack of sleep tightened the muscles in Colton's neck, and he reached around to rub the tense places. Maybe he'd find time for a nap this afternoon.

Try as he might, he couldn't convince himself to leave the thoughts of Auralie Covington behind. According to Barnabas, he needed to get himself hitched and have a passel of young'uns. Colton snorted. Even if he had time for a woman in his life, it certainly wouldn't be Shelby Covington's daughter. The ludicrous thought reproached him.

Dogwood trees winked their white blossoms at the spring sky, rhododendrons unfolded their flowers in celebration of the new day, and purple violets dotted the shaded slopes. A wagon carrying a family loomed up ahead, and rather than risk the wheels splashing mud up on his polished boots or clean britches, Colton slowed the gelding to ride at a safe distance behind. The four children in the back of the wagon—two boys and two girls, all dressed

in their Sunday best—laughed and teased each other and
made up a silly song as they rolled down the road. The children's parents turned around and smiled at the young ones
and joined in the laughter. The scene stirred a longing in
Colton's chest. Perhaps God had a family in store for him
some day, but not now.

The church bell pealed through the trees. Colton hated
arriving at church late, but a pang of disappointment
pinched him when the father whistled to the team to hurry
them along, ending Colton's enjoyment of watching the
children. He followed the family into the churchyard and
found a shady spot to tether Jasper. A few other folks arrived and exchanged greetings. At least he wouldn't be
the only one walking in just as the bell ceased its tolling.
He searched for a seat before Pastor Shuford stepped into
the pulpit.

Colton smiled at the other members of the congregation
around him—hardworking people like himself who observed the Lord's Day by gathering together in the simple
church. He turned to glance across the aisle. Auralie Covington sat beside Belle Hancock. Surprise blinked through
him. He knew she'd been visiting her cousin, but it didn't
occur to him that a woman like her might attend church in
this modest little house of worship, even though the Hancocks attended regularly. Before he could discipline his
focus, Auralie turned and their gazes collided.

He sent her a polite nod and forced his attention to the
front where the pastor announced the first hymn. But halfway through "How Firm a Foundation" he caught himself
sliding his gaze sideways while everyone else had their
faces buried in their hymnbooks. Everyone else except Auralie. The moment their eyes met for the second time, her
face flooded with color and she quickly looked back at
her songbook.

Heat filled his face, and he wondered what Pastor Shuford must think. He glanced up to see if the preacher had witnessed the exchange. Judging by the twinkle in the man's eye when he looked straight at Colton, he'd not only noticed, he'd been amused.

After three more hymns, the congregation was seated, and Colton admonished himself to anchor his attention on the sermon. But the knowledge of Auralie's presence crept in, taunting his thoughts.

Lord, why am I doing this? I can't be attracted to a woman like Auralie Covington. I'll only make a fool of myself if I keep looking at her. She's of a completely different class. I'm a farmer and shepherd. She's an aristocrat. Please take these unreasonable feelings for her away from me.

Pastor Shuford instructed the congregation to turn to Joshua, chapter one. As he led the worshippers in reading the scripture, the verses Colton had heard a hundred times spoke to him in a way he'd never before considered. Hearing the preacher proclaim with assurance that God would be with him as He was with Moses, that God would not fail him or forsake him, left Colton breathless. What a precious promise. Was such a promise meant for someone like him? A simple farmer? Could he be a Joshua? Colton attuned his heart to drink up the preaching of God's Word.

Like many of the promises in the Bible, this one came with a command. *"Be strong and of a good courage."* The very words drew a picture of unwavering trust in the One who promised to always be with him. If God loved him enough to never forsake him regardless of the circumstances, then God believed he had a place in this world, a place of significance. Otherwise, why would He waste His time?

The message spilled over Colton in much the same way

Pastor Winslow's encouragement did. Be strong and of good courage. The admonition that rang in his ears carried with it a thread of warning as well. Events were unfolding around the bend in the road, beyond the horizon where he could not see, but God's promise meant He was already there, and Colton need not fear the unseen or unknown. Heeding God's command to be strong and courageous meant fortifying his heart and reinforcing his foundation of trust.

It never occurred to Auralie that she'd run into Colton at the little church her cousin attended, but she wasn't really surprised to learn he was a churchgoing man. His public statements, urging people to pray and seek God's will before supporting a candidate or casting a ballot fell into line with watching him sit in rapt attention of the preacher's sermon. The way he'd spoken of the land and his sheep the other day—like they were blessings, gifts from the hand of God—left her feeling a bit ashamed for never realizing the value God placed on hard work. Colton regarded the work of his hands as a gift, not drudgery, with peace and contentment rather than resentment. Such a man piqued her curiosity. She'd certainly never seen her father dirty his hands. In fact, more than once she'd heard him speak of working people with disdain. Even though she'd not set eyes on Perry Bolden since they were children, she suspected her fiancé leaned toward her father's notions.

She sneaked several peeks at Colton during the service. His demeanor intrigued her. She'd grown up thinking sitting in a worship service was a stiff, formal affair. Colton's profile was etched with an emotion she'd not seen in a man before. In fact, the only other person she recalled seeing with a similar expression was Mammy. When Mammy read from the Bible and when she talked about the Lord, she did so with pure adoration in her eyes. Auralie glimpsed that same worshipful countenance on Colton. He hung on every word the pastor said, even brushing a tear or two from his eye.

Auralie had known from childhood what it meant to trust Christ for salvation, but watching Colton absorb the preacher's words about God's promises pricked her with envy. Was this what Belle meant when she inquired why Auralie would be afraid of a God who loved her?

The rugged lines of Colton's jaw captured her attention. For almost four years, she'd tried to remember what Perry Bolden looked like. As her gaze traced the shadow of Colton's profile, she realized with a start that she hadn't wondered about Perry's appearance in weeks, and she didn't feel the least bit guilty about it. This man, unlike any other she'd ever met, was work toughened and tender at the same time. He showed gratitude for what God had given him and worked hard to care for it. Above everything else, he humbled himself in a way she'd never seen a man do before. This was the embodiment of a real man—not the kind of man who stepped over people to get what he wanted, or used money and power to manipulate his circumstances, not one who lorded over others or talked down to them.

Colton shifted his position, uncrossing and recrossing his legs. He glanced in her direction, and a tiny smile twitched his lips when he caught her looking at him. A flutter tickled her stomach, and she pulled her gaze back where it belonged, but not before returning his smile.

A gentle nudge poked her ribs. Belle covered her mouth with her fingers and coughed. When Auralie looked up at her cousin, an odd expression filled Belle's eyes. Heat rushed up Auralie's neck and chagrin filled her. The announcement of her engagement to Perry Bolden was scheduled within a few weeks, and here she sat in church, experiencing flutters and exchanging smiles with Colton Danfield. The word *hussy* tiptoed through her mind and fanned the flames in her cheeks.

"Your pastor must think I'm some kind of heathen." Auralie covered her face with her hands as they rode home in the carriage. A fresh wave of discomfort washed over her. "I couldn't even look him in the eye when he shook my hand at the door."

Belle giggled. "If you had, you would have seen that he was smiling." She grasped Auralie's hand. "It could have been worse. You might have fallen asleep and started snoring."

"Belle!" Auralie glanced up at Sam driving the carriage and saw his shoulders shake silently.

A wicked grin worked its way into Belle's face. "One time a man—I think he was a deacon—went to sleep and fell forward and hit his head on the pew in front of him. They had to carry him out." Her cousin stroked her chin. "Then there was the time—"

"Belle, it's not funny. I was mortified. What if this gets back to my father?"

"I doubt there is anyone from our little church who is on casual speaking terms with Uncle Shelby." Belle shrugged. "Except maybe Jack McCaffey."

Auralie spun in her seat, her eyes wide. "The editor of the newspaper? Oh, I think I'm going to be sick."

Belle emitted a tinkling laugh. "I was kidding. He wasn't even there today." She turned sideways and grasped Auralie's shoulders. "Relax. I was just trying to make you see the funny side of this." She rocked back and forth with laughter.

"Oh of course. It's sidesplitting." She lifted her eyes heavenward. "You always did have an odd sense of humor."

She took off her gloves and fanned herself with them. "I shall never forgive you for teasing me."

Belle wiped tears from her face. "Don't you remember the time we had a contest to see which of us could climb a tree faster and I got stuck and your brother had to get me down? You teased me about that for months. I'm simply paying you back."

"That was more than ten years ago!" Auralie batted her cousin with her gloves. "How long do you hold a grudge?"

Hoofbeats sounded behind them. Sam steered the horses to move the carriage over so the rider could pass, but instead the chestnut horse pulled up alongside.

"Mrs. Hancock. Miss Covington."

Sam slowed the carriage, and Auralie turned at the sound of the familiar voice. Her breath strangled in her throat and all that came out was a squeak.

Amusement threaded Belle's voice. "Hello, Mr. Danfield. We don't see much of you, even though you are our nearest neighbor."

Auralie wanted to return the favor and elbow her cousin in the ribs. She managed a smile and polite nod, but her face flamed.

Mr. Danfield removed his hat. "I missed paying my respects to you ladies at church. When the service ends, it's often difficult to speak to everyone." His warm eyes locked with Auralie's. "Miss Covington, I wanted to tell you again how much we appreciated the lemonade."

Belle cocked her head and gave Auralie a curious look, her eyebrows arching like a pair of hissing cats.

Auralie found her voice. "It was my pleasure, Mr. Danfield. I'm glad you enjoyed it."

Belle's lips pressed together as if she was trying to keep from bursting into laughter. "Mr. Danfield, I feel I've been remiss. We've been neighbors for almost three years, and

I've yet to extend an invitation to dinner. We would be pleased to have you join us this afternoon for Sunday dinner. I heard Maizie say she was preparing a roast."

Auralie tried to swallow and nearly choked. She wanted to shake her cousin. What in heaven's name did she think she was doing? Surely Mr. Danfield would see through Belle's ploy as nothing more than a matchmaking scheme and refuse the invitation.

Surprise flickered over Mr. Danfield's features, and he hesitated. His eyes shifted from Belle to Auralie, and the same tiny smile he sent across the aisle at church tweaked his lips again. Pleasure danced in his eyes.

"Why, that's very gracious of you, Mrs. Hancock. I really must go home first to check on—" He glanced downward for a moment, then smiled. "There are a few things that require my attention, but I would be pleased to accept. What time should I be there?"

A smile sweet enough to melt butter graced Belle's face. "Around one o'clock would be perfect."

He slid his gaze to Auralie. "I shall look forward to it." He replaced his hat and tugged on the brim. "Until later, ladies." He nudged his horse into a canter.

"Belle…" Auralie lowered her voice to a growl.

"Don't Belle me." A smirk danced through Belle's eyes. "What is this about lemonade?"

Chapter 9

"**I** must be losing my mind."

Colton muttered to himself all the way home. Whatever possessed him to accept Mrs. Hancock's dinner invitation? True, she was a neighbor, but judging by the mischief that twinkled in her eyes and the way Miss Covington's eyes widened like she was facing the gallows, he'd just stepped into something better left alone.

Images of Auralie Covington kept him awake half the night, and he'd adamantly instructed himself to remain aloof. Seeing her at church took him by surprise, and he berated himself for repeatedly looking her way. Now he could only surmise that his brain had taken a holiday. What was he thinking?

Was it proper to have accepted the invitation to the Hancock home since Lloyd was away? It wasn't as if Mrs. Hancock was there alone, but he had a suspicion the invitation was more of a nudge to get to know Miss Covington rather than a neighborly gesture.

Barnabas met him in the yard by the barn as soon as he rode up. He took Jasper's reins while Colton dismounted.

"Mistah Colton, you look like yo' best frien' just up and died. Don' you know you s'posed to come home from church wi' th' joy o' the Lawd in yo' heart and on yo' face?"

Colton hung his head. "I did something stupid."

A soft snort reached his ears, and he looked up to find Barnabas rubbing his hand over his mouth. "Mistah Colton, yo's a lot o' things, but stupid ain't one of 'em." He started to lead the horse into the barn.

"Don't unsaddle him. Just give him some water and a little bit of hay." Colton took off the preacher's coat and folded it carefully over his arm. "I've been invited to Sunday dinner."

Barnabas bobbed his head. "That be right nice."

"But I *accepted* the invitation."

"I don' understand." Barnabas planted a hand on his hip. "Ain't that what yo's s'posed to do?"

Colton ran his hand over his forehead and pulled his hat off. "Well, yes. Normally it would be a very nice thing to do. But in this case, I'm having dinner with our neighbor, Mrs. Hancock, and her cousin, Miss Auralie Covington."

Barnabas's eyes crinkled into merriment. "Then I didn' make no mistake. That be right nice." He led the horse into the barn and tethered him.

"That depends on your perspective—how you look at it." Colton shook his head. "Having dinner with Miss Covington is like smacking a hornet's nest with a big stick."

Barnabas dipped a bucketful of water for the horse and deposited a small mound of hay in front of him. "I agree wi' you 'bout one thing. Smackin' a hornet's nest sho' be a stupid thing to do. But how can settin' down to dinner wit' a pretty lady be stupid?"

The two men walked side by side from the barn to the house. "She's Shelby Covington's daughter." Stating what Barnabas already knew didn't clear up the muddy water. Colton wasn't sure he could put into words what he didn't want to hear with his own ears, much less speak to another man.

"Barnabas, don't you see? She comes from an important, powerful, wealthy family. Her father is running for governor, and I detest most of the things he stands for. She's been raised in luxury and privilege. I was raised learning the value of hard work. I'm nothing but a farmer and shepherd." He turned to face the man who once toiled as a slave for Auralie's father. "I have forty acres of land that I sweat over with your help. Covington Plantation is nearly a thousand acres that uses over a hundred slaves to work. Sitting at dinner with the likes of Auralie Covington would be akin to tramping into the palace of Queen Victoria with muddy boots."

Barnabas dipped his head and rubbed his stubbly chin. Colton never noticed before how gray Barnabas was getting. He'd never even thought to ask how old the man was or if he'd ever fallen in love or had a family. The realization pinched a nerve in Colton's heart and shamed him.

"Mistah Colton, is you tryin' to tell me you ain't good enough to have dinner wi' Miz Covington? 'Cause that jus' ain't so. You is a man who loves God and always try to live in a way that please Him. You know what right and wrong, and you stand up fo' it. You ain't never hurt no one that I knows about. Yo's honest an' a man can trus' what yo' say." Barnabas's voice cracked. "An' you save my life, Mistah Colton. Them overseers woulda killed me fo' sho' iffen I'd stayed there too much longer. You give me my freedom and dignity, lettin' me work like a man oughta work, takin' pride in what he do, an' earnin' his way in dis here world." He shook his head. "No, Mistah Colton, I cain't let you say you ain't good enough. I'd go to fightin' any man who say you ain't good enough. You the bes' man I evah know."

In all the time Colton had known him, Barnabas had never made a speech before. Colton didn't know what to say. He'd grown up with the encouragement of godly parents, and Pastor Winslow was as dear to him as anyone in this world. The old preacher taught him by example what it meant to have a servant's heart. What Barnabas just said to him was exactly how he felt about Pastor Winslow.

His throat tightened, and he must have gotten something in his eye. Dust, no doubt.

He clapped his hand on Barnabas's shoulder, holding it there for several long moments. The two men spoke without uttering a word.

Colton cleared his throat. "I think I'll go freshen up."

Barnabas took the preacher's coat from Colton. He hung it on the peg and began brushing it meticulously. A smile creased Colton's face.

Colton politely held Mrs. Hancock's chair as his hostess was seated. "Thank you, again, for the invitation. It's been a while since I sat at such a nice table."

Miss Covington seated herself at the opposite side of the table, and Colton gritted his teeth at his inability to move quickly enough to hold her chair as well. Her soft smile made him catch his breath.

She reminded him of a cameo brooch that belonged to his mother. He used to stare at it when he was little boy, thinking the lady whose ivory profile appeared there surely must be the most beautiful woman in the world, next to his mother, of course. Manhood had changed his perspective, and Auralie Covington now rivaled every other woman he envisioned, including the woman on his mother's cameo brooch.

The black woman Mrs. Hancock called Maizie set bowls of savory vegetables and a platter of succulent roast beef on the table. Miss Covington's mammy carried a tureen heaped with mashed potatoes and a pitcher of gravy and set them near the head of the table, while a man called Sam filled the glasses.

"Mr. Danfield, will you please ask the blessing?"

Colton smiled. "It would be my honor." He bowed his head and lifted his voice to the throne room of God, asking special favor on this house and those who lived under its roof and the hands that labored to prepare the meal. Finally, he asked God to bless the food to nourish and strengthen them, thanking God for His provision, mercy, and grace.

When they said amen and raised their heads, Colton caught a glimpse of Miss Covington's wide brown eyes reflecting wonder. Didn't she think he knew how to pray?

As they passed the dishes and platters, Colton turned to his hostess. "What do you hear from Lloyd?"

While Mrs. Hancock recounted Lloyd's last letter, Colton forced himself to pay attention to his hostess's report, but the sweet distraction sitting across from him tested his willpower. "It sounds as if he has made an impression on the senior heads of the firm in Atlanta. You must be very proud of him."

"Oh, I am. But I miss him terribly." Mrs. Hancock took a sip from her glass. "I'm hoping he can come home be-fore—" She cleared her throat. "Before too long."

Colton took a deep breath. Barnabas declared him "good enough" to sit at dinner with Miss Covington. The least he should do is include her in the conversation. "Miss Covington, it's so good of you to keep your cousin company while Lloyd is away."

She'd done little more than push the food around on her plate. Was she uncomfortable with him sitting across from her? Perhaps she didn't agree with Barnabas's view. He gave himself a mental kick. He shouldn't have come. He should have…

A smile filled her eyes when she looked up. "I am the one who is the beneficiary. I love it here. If I could, I'd stay indefinitely."

Her statement surprised him. While the Hancocks weren't poor by any means, they didn't possess the wealth reflected on the Covington Plantation. She picked up the basket of biscuits and handed it to Colton.

"I was walking in the meadow the other day, watching the lambs in your pasture." A charming expression lit her eyes. "They're so adorable."

"You must come over and get a closer look at them some time." The invitation fell out of his mouth before he could snatch it back.

"Perhaps."

Change the subject, you fool. "Have you and your cousin always been close?"

Mrs. Hancock managed a mischievous grin, but Miss Covington responded with a look of exasperation. "Yes, but my cousin can be a terrible tease at times."

Mrs. Hancock's eyes twinkled. "Ah, but we laugh a lot."

The very idea of laughing with Auralie Covington filled Colton with a notion of such pleasure he dared not try to define it.

Auralie stood beside Belle at the front door and watched Colton Danfield ride off toward his house. Misgivings disturbed her better judgment when she admitted—albeit only to herself—that she'd enjoyed the time spent with Mr. Danfield.

"See, that wasn't so bad, was it?" Belle closed the door and arched her eyebrows at Auralie.

"Belle..." Auralie brushed her hand across her forehead. "What do you think you're doing? I'm *engaged* to be married."

"To a man you don't love and didn't choose." Belle looped her arm through Auralie's as they walked away from the door. "And the engagement hasn't been formally announced yet, so it's perfectly proper to have a simple meal with a neighbor in the presence of a chaperone." She waved her fingers in a swooping motion at herself, indicating her presence ensured the afternoon had been completely appropriate. "All I'm trying to do is make you visualize how it could be if you were to do your own choosing."

A sigh, festered on despair, rose into Auralie's throat. "But that privilege has been taken away from me."

Belle gave a soft snort. "Whatever happened to my feisty cousin who dared to dream about the impossible? Think about it, Auralie. What's the worst that can happen if you refuse to marry Perry Bolden?"

Refuse? The word smacked Auralie in the face. The very idea of refusing her father's demands sent a shudder through her.

Belle stifled a yawn. "While you're thinking about it, I'm going upstairs to take a nap. Care to do likewise?"

"No thanks." Auralie gave her cousin a quick hug. She couldn't very well blame Belle for meddling when all she'd done was invite a neighbor to dinner. "You know, you've always been more like a sister to me than a cousin."

"I know. And you got me in trouble more times than I can count when we were children." A wicked gleam glittered in Belle's eye. "That's why I can get away with playing matchmaker." She giggled and headed for the stairs.

"Belle!"

Auralie shook her head. Belle meant no harm, and truth be told, she loved her cousin for what she was trying to do. But stirring up desires she'd buried long ago was a dangerous thing when her father was involved.

She headed for her favorite rocker on the side porch and curled up. Once comfortable, she realized she'd forgotten to bring the copy of *Wuthering Heights* with her, and she didn't feel like going back into the house after it. She snuggled into the cushions and laid her head back. Without anything to read, her mind lay vulnerable to imaginings.

Belle prodded her to remember the adventurous childhood they'd spent, when Auralie was usually the one to dare Belle into taking chances. Now it seemed things were turned around.

Belle's question rang in her ears. What *was* the worst that could happen? In the fairy tales she'd read as a child, the beautiful princess was locked up in a tower, but locking her up wasn't what her father wanted. His intention was for her to be on display, like Belle's china dolls—an elegant, graceful woman who exuded the lifestyle, kept her mouth shut, and hung on her husband's arm like an ornament.

When one was raised in a culture in which crossing class lines was unconventional, breaking such a tradition shook her foundation. She let her eyes drift closed and the image that came to mind was Colton Danfield sitting in church, intently listening to God's Word preached, wiping away a tear, saturating himself with the presence of God.

Had she ever done that? She believed in God and had trusted Christ as a child. But there was something missing in her faith. Mammy had tried to make her see it, and Belle had hinted Auralie's relationship with God was lacking. But she didn't understand until she watched Colton Danfield sit in awe and pure adoration of the God he loved.

Conviction.

That's the word that described what she saw in Colton, not only in the way he viewed God, but in the way he lived his life.

What convictions could she claim? Did she have that level of belief that God loved her and kept His promises? Despite having just finished eating Sunday dinner, she felt ravaged by hunger, but not a hunger for anything tangible. What she longed for was a filling of unshakable hope that she could cling to God in utter and unspoiled trust. That's what she saw in Colton Danfield. Everything about him bespoke of a deeply rooted conviction that God remain enthroned in the very center of his life.

She'd never witnessed such a faith from her father. The motive for everything her father did was greed and lust for power. When she'd questioned almost two years ago why Perry wrote to her father rather than to her, she was harshly silenced and told to stay in her place. A month ago she'd finally received a letter from Perry, and he hadn't mentioned God one time, but rather communicated the same dictatorial air she'd grown accustomed to seeing in her father.

She opened her eyes and raised them to the puffy, white clouds that drifted lazily across the blue sky. Last night's storm had rattled the walls and roof like a demonic thing seeking to devour her. Today, the cornflower blue skies, wispy clouds, and balmy breeze defined how God could keep her through the storm. Not all storms were comprised of slashing lightning, booming thunder, and wild winds. Some storms raged in the heart. Could God calm a storm within the same way He'd sheltered her during the treacherous lightning and crashing thunder?

Chapter 10

Colton stared at the colorful banner flapping in the breeze, declaring Shelby Covington the best candidate for governor. It stretched the entire width of the main street, from the lamppost next to the courthouse across the street to the saloon. Colton shook his head in disgust. The accolades borne on the banner were a stretch at best and fabrications in reality.

Clyde Sawyer stepped out the mercantile doors and stood next to Colton, hands on hips and a scowl twisting his gray whiskers. He pointed to the pretentious sign. "Is that a joke?"

"No. Covington is running for governor." Colton did his best to disguise his personal dislike of the man. Being asked to speak on behalf of local small farmers at a private gathering was one thing, but he'd not make a spectacle of himself on the street, publicly denouncing a candidate.

Clyde flapped his hand like he was shooing away an annoying gnat. "I mean that other stuff." He splayed his fingers and waved his hand in a grand arc imitating the size of the banner. "Best man for the job? A man you can trust?" Clyde's voice rang with contempt. He angled his head and looked sideways at Colton. "That's the biggest crock of—"

"Clyde?" Betsy's shrill voice carried from inside the mercantile.

The merchant cast a look of mock exasperation heavenward. "I'll be there in a minute, Sweet Pea," he called out before turning back to Colton. "So what brings you to town in the middle of the week?"

Colton pulled a scrap of paper from his shirt pocket and handed it to Clyde. "Just need a few things. I have to pick up some feed and a couple of rolls of fencing from Sloan Talbot. I'm enlarging the chicken coop. Can I pick up those supplies on my way back?"

"Sure thing." Clyde leaned closer. "Say, did you hear the news. Stephen Douglas got the most votes at the Democratic Convention, but he didn't win a clear majority. They say there was quite a rhubarb going on down there in Charleston. Fussin' and fightin' to beat the band."

Colton slapped his hat back on his head. "I was planning on picking up this week's edition of the *Sentinel* today. There ought to be something in there about the goings-on in Charleston."

Clyde dug a nickel out of his pocket and held it out. "Pick up a copy for me, will you?"

"*Clyyyyde!*" Betsy screeched for her husband again. "Where did you get off to? I need your help."

A wide grin stretched Colton's face. "You're going to be in trouble if you don't go see what she wants."

"You're right." Clyde chuckled. "Just between you and me, sometimes I think she enjoys getting all in a flutter." He raised his voice a few notches. "*Coming, Sweet Pea.*"

He turned and waved. "Talk to you later, Colton. Oh, Betsy made some strawberry preserves and she wants to give you a jar, so remind me when you—"

"*Clyde Sawyer!* Do I have to come lookin' for you?"

Clyde beat a hasty retreat back inside, and Colton climbed aboard the wagon seat. He whistled to the team and headed off toward Talbot's Feed and Seed. The enterprise's owner—the man with whom Colton had exchanged words the week before—stood on the loading platform, counting stacked burlap sacks.

Sloan gave him a cool nod. "What can I do for you, Colton?" His tone bore a thread of malice, left over from their previous encounter, no doubt.

Colton climbed down from the high seat. "Morning, Sloan. Nice day, isn't it?"

A scowl wormed its way across Sloan's brow. "Haven't had time to notice. You need somethin'?"

If the man didn't want to be civil, there was nothing Colton could do about it. "I need a hundred pounds of oats, a hundred of barley, and two hundred of cracked corn. Do you have any of that crushed sorghum cane?"

Sloan gave a short nod. "How much you want?"

"A hundred pounds of the crushed cane, and a roll of poultry netting." He pulled his wallet out of his pocket.

Sloan's frown deepened. "Don't you want to put this on your account?"

Colton shook his head. "Cash on the barrel. I trust the prices are still the same?"

A rush of red filled Sloan's face and he jerked his head toward a crudely lettered sign hanging against the board and batten siding. "Price chart is right there."

Without giving the list more than a cursory glance, Colton pulled a few bills from his wallet and extended them to Sloan. The man who Colton once called a friend snatched the money, stuffed it in his pocket, and stomped into the warehouse to fetch the purchased sacks of grain.

Colton sighed. He remembered Pastor Winslow telling him once that sometimes all a man has that he can call his own are his principles. If taking a stand against secession, and more specifically against slavery, caused Sloan to cut friendship ties with him, then so be it.

Sloan dumped the heavy sacks on the platform and let Colton load them himself.

Colton set the brake and tethered the team outside the mercantile, but before going inside to pick up his supplies, he jogged across the street to the *Juniper Springs Sentinel* office and bought two copies of the latest edition. He exchanged greetings with the editor, Jack McCaffey, and wandered out the door reading the headline.

Covington Promises Rail Service if Elected

Reading as he ambled back toward the mercantile, he collided with a man and dropped Clyde's copy of the paper he'd tucked under his arm.

He jerked his head up. "Oh, excuse me. I'm sorry."

The gentleman in the fine gray frock coat and silver brocade vest scowled and brushed imaginary dirt from his sleeve. "Watch where you're going." He straightened his silk maroon paisley cravat and proceeded to his waiting carriage, stepping on Clyde's dropped newspaper in the process.

Familiarity rang in the man's face and voice. Colton had seen him before but couldn't recall when or where. The landau carriage, with its crest-adorned door and polished brass lamps, pulled away. Colton glanced up at the sign over the door the man had just exited. The land office.

"Not very polite, is he?"

Colton turned his attention to the one making the comment. Cyrus Fletcher, Juniper Springs' only lawyer, sent a derisive frown after the carriage and bent to pick up the newspaper, brushing off some of the dirt before handing it back to Colton.

"Thanks." Colton glanced at the soiled paper. It wasn't ruined, but he switched it with the paper he'd been reading, intending to give the clean copy to Clyde Sawyer. "No, I'd say the gentleman definitely lacked manners. Do you know that fellow?"

Cyrus snorted. "I wish I didn't. That's Maxwell Rayburn, Esq."

Colton pondered the name. "Wasn't he that fancy attorney from Athens you went up against a time or two?"

"That's right. That land right-of-way case a few years ago. Shelby Covington sued to prevent local farmers from using a trail they'd used for years because it went through the tract where he was building his brickworks. The farmers weren't damaging anything—they were just passing through on their way to transport their harvested crops downriver. The trail was the easiest and straightest way, but Covington denied them access. Rayburn pulled a dirty trick or two out of his sleeve, the court ruled in Covington's favor, and the farmers suffered." Cyrus looked in the direction the fancy carriage had taken, then at the building Rayburn had exited. "Wonder what he's doing up here."

Auralie trembled and paused halfway down the stairs. A man she didn't know stood beside the bottom step with one hand on the ornately swirled rail. The harsh glare of light behind him made his features impossible to distinguish. She hesitated, her feet frozen in place on the stairs. Every instinct told her to dash back up the stairs, run to her room, and bolt the door behind her.

"Come." His voice sounded far away and he held out his hand.

Panic spiraled within her, but her full, sweeping skirts of pink silk hampered her movements. She sent a frantic look over her shoulder. Mammy stood at the top of the stairs, shaking her head and wiping a tear away with the corner of her apron.

"Come." The voice sounded closer and more commanding.

Auralie jerked her head around. No longer at the halfway point on the stairs, she now stood three-fourths of the way down without having moved her feet an inch. Who was this man ordering her about? His chin lifted and he held his head at an arrogant angle. With outstretched fingers, he beckoned. Beyond the mysterious figure, Colton Danfield stood near the door, his hat in one hand. His other hand extended to her as well, but in a gentle, inviting manner, as if offering her a choice.

Her chest constricted, and it was hard to breathe. She realized her corset was laced much too tightly. Heat rushed into her face. When she looked down at herself, the pink silk was gone. In its place was a pearl-studded gown of white satin and Chantilly lace. A veil of matching lace cascaded from her head across her arms. A droplet trickled down her face. Was it perspiration? Or a tear?

The glaring light outside disappeared and inky blackness blanketed them. A ferocious flare of lightning blazed from the windows, illuminating the face of the man waiting for her at the foot of the stairs. His downturned mouth and sinister, narrowed eyes sent a jolt of fear through her. He pointed to her and then slowly drew a path with his finger, directing her to come and stand beside him. She sent a desperate glance beyond him toward the door, where

Colton stood, but he'd vanished. Why didn't she grasp his outstretched hand while she had the chance?

"Come!" The imposing tone pronounced the single word as if it were an edict handed down from a king to his subjects.

A deafening crash of thunder made her grab her skirts and turn to scurry up the stairs, but at that moment a vise-like grip encircled her arm with such force, she cried out. Clawing at the hand in a vain attempt to escape, she sought the face of the one who held her. Shelby Covington glowered down at her and pulled her by her arm down the stairs toward the man who waited for her.

"Father, please don't make me do this." The plea tore from her throat.

Beside him, her mother stood dressed entirely in black, fluttering a fan, a passive nonexpression on her face.

"Father..."

"Wake up, chile."

Auralie's eyes flew open, and she bolted upright with a gasp. She sat amid tangled bedcovers. A single candle flickered on the bedside table. Sweat dripped from her hair, and she sucked in great gulps of air. Mammy leaned over her, drawing Auralie into her arms.

"Yo's havin' a bad dream, honey girl. Jes' a dream, that all it is, jes' a dream. Mmm-hmm." Mammy hummed in that familiar, soothing voice she'd used to comfort Auralie for as long as she could remember. "Shh, now. Yo's gonna rouse the whole house wit' yo' hollerin'."

Auralie sagged into Mammy's embrace, relief quivering through her. She lifted her trembling hands and clung to the sweet Negro woman like she used to do as a child. Mammy continued to hum, a spiritual Auralie had heard her sing a thousand times, as she gently rocked back and forth and stroked Auralie's damp hair.

After several minutes, Mammy took Auralie's shoulders. "Honey girl, you all right now?"

"Yes." Discomfort scraped her raspy throat. "Better now. I'm sorry I awakened you."

"Nonsense, chile." The thin glow of the candle danced across Mammy's face as she retrieved a towel from the washstand. She began patting Auralie's face and neck, brushing back the damp tendrils of hair. "There now. I's jus' goin' to sit right here beside you while you fall back to sleep."

"No, Mammy. You need your sleep, and I think I want to stay awake for a while longer." She swung her feet to the floor and reached for her dressing gown.

Candlelight outlined the concern in Mammy's eyes. "Honey girl? When you was dreamin', you cried out to the Father." She stroked Auralie's hair. "Was you prayin'?"

Mammy's question jolted her. Praying? "No, I wasn't. But I think it's time I started."

Auralie and Belle relaxed on the east-facing side porch where the morning sun peeked through the trees and sent rays of dappled light skittering across the tabletop. Belle's morning nausea had eased up some, and she nibbled on a piece of cinnamon toast.

"Do you think you could eat some strawberries?" Auralie offered the bowl to her cousin. "Try one."

Belle made a face. "I think I'd better stay with the toast and tea."

"That's not much of a breakfast," Auralie admonished. "Maizie and Mammy said you're supposed to be eating for two."

Belle grinned. "I'll make up for it later."

Fragrant honeysuckle scented the air, and a nearby pair of squirrels bickered over the rights to a pinecone. The late spring breeze waved the tree limbs in an impromptu waltz. The idyllic setting soothed the tension from last night's dream from Auralie's shoulders. She took another sip of coffee. This place had become her refuge, far removed from the impending reality that had prompted last night's terror. She drew in a breath and let it out slowly, easing her head back against the wicker chair's cushion and letting her eyes drift closed.

"I have an idea."

Auralie opened her eyes.

Belle's expression sparkled with anticipation. "Let's go into Juniper Springs to the dry goods store and look at material for sewing a layette for the baby. I'm going to need yards and yards of flannel for diapers, and maybe you could help me make some simple little gowns." She clasped her hands together under her chin, fingers interlaced. "Why don't we stop and see if Frances Hyatt could make something special for the baby. A christening gown, perhaps?"

Enthusiasm sparked within Auralie. "Oh, that sounds like such fun. Why don't we look for some cloth to make a little quilt? Since the baby isn't coming until fall, he—or she—will need a warm quilt."

Belle rose and pulled Auralie to her feet. "Let's go get ready. I'll tell Sam to hitch up the carriage, and we'll go right away."

Delight tickled Auralie's stomach, and she scurried inside and up the stairs to freshen up. Mammy came to repin her hair into a snood so it wouldn't tumble in disarray during the carriage ride.

"I hope the dry goods store has a good supply of flannel." Auralie grinned while Mammy dressed her hair. "Making sweet little things for the baby will be so much fun."

A tap at Auralie's bedroom door drew their attention.

"Miss Auralie?" Maizie nudged the door open. "This just now come fo' you." She held out a folded missive.

The very sight of the paper in Maizie's hand sucked the breath from Auralie's lungs. Her heart hammered against her ribs, and she twisted her ring while whispering a prayer. "Please, Lord, don't let it be what I think it is." Fighting to draw a deep, steadying breath, she took the note. "Thank you, Maizie." Her name was written on the outside in her mother's unmistakable flowing script. With trembling hands, she broke the seal and unfolded the paper.

Auralie,
Mrs. Gabrielle Bolden is coming from Athens to visit on Tuesday, the twenty-second of May for the purpose of discussing the planning of your engagement ball. Her plans indicate she will stay through Thursday. Your presence is, of course, required. A carriage will be sent Monday morning, the twenty-first of May, immediately after breakfast to bring you home. Your father will see you upon your return.
Mother

Chapter 11

Auralie tiptoed out of Belle's room and quietly closed the door. Just when they thought her morning sickness had abated, another bout of nausea seized her cousin this morning.

Sympathy tugged at Auralie's heart for the poor girl. She'd finally fallen asleep after Auralie bathed her face and opened the window to allow the cool breeze coming off the mountain to enter. She descended the stairs and exited through the back door. The aroma of fresh bread greeted her at the door of the summer kitchen where she found Maizie and Mammy. "Belle is asleep. I'm going to go for a walk."

She followed the stone walkway that led past the vegetable garden where Sam worked. He nodded politely as she passed. She rounded the corner of the house by the east-facing side porch where she liked curling up with a book. But today, not even *Wuthering Heights* held any appeal.

Her mother's note and the anticipation of having to face

Mrs. Bolden stole the usual joy with which she entered each day here at Belle's house. What if her future mother-in-law expected her to have detailed plans for the soiree? Other than writing a list of invitees that Perry had demanded, she'd given no thought to the upcoming event other than to dread its arrival.

She bent to pluck a clover blossom and twirl it between her thumb and forefinger. Her time would be better spent sitting at the desk in her upstairs room, making assorted lists to appease her mother and Mrs. Bolden, but drinking in the freedom of the beautiful day felt far more pressing.

The split rail fence of black locust marked the edge of the yard. She wandered past it, searching the meadow in the distance to see if the lambs were cavorting as she'd seen them do on other days.

"Mr. Danfield said I should come over and get a closer look at them." She only hesitated a moment. In a few weeks, the privilege of choice would be stripped away and she'd be in bondage, just like her mother. Today, she intended to do as she pleased.

The meadow grasses swayed in the breeze, ebbing and swelling much like the ocean billows she'd once seen. The motion eased her mind back to her childhood when she twirled and danced to the music she made up in her head. Those carefree days, spent without thought of what she'd have to endure later in life, etched sweet memories on her soul. Did her mother have similar memories? If she did, she'd never shared them. Perhaps those secret recollections were what sustained her mother now.

She neared the fence line of the Danfield farm and searched the shady slopes for the lambs. A handful of mother sheep grazed while their offspring either played or slept. Mr. Danfield was right. They were even cuter close up than when looking at them from a distance.

The same black-and-white dog she'd seen on her previous visit paced back and forth between the sheep grazing at the bottom of the hill and a secluded spot at the crest of the slope. He seemed friendly enough, but Auralie wondered if he'd mind her coming into the pasture. She carefully gathered her skirts and climbed over the fence. The dog perked up his ears and barked a couple of times but made no aggressive moves. She stood still to see if any of the lambs might approach her.

The wind calmed and plaintive bleating sounded. The dog whined and dashed back up to the top of the slope. Curious, Auralie followed.

Just beyond the crest, a plump sheep lay, periodically thrashing its legs and emitting a pitiful *baa*. Auralie crept closer and peered at the ewe that seemed in obvious distress.

Auralie looked around for signs of Mr. Danfield or his helper but could see neither. Kneeling in the deep grass, she reached a tentative hand to stroke the sheep's head. "Poor thing. Are you sick?"

The animal grunted, its doleful bleats raking across Auralie's heart. Alarmed that the sheep might be in trouble, she stood and swept her gaze across the area as far as she could see. Only the nearest portion of the cornfield was visible from where she stood. Perhaps Mr. Danfield was working on the far end of the field. She picked up her skirt and hurried down the slope.

The dog followed her but halted where the other sheep grazed and didn't appear to want to leave them. Auralie's toe caught her hem, and she stumbled and fell face-first in the meadow grass, knocking the air from her lungs. She struggled to her hands and knees, sucking in as much air as she could before getting to her feet. Dirt and grass stains marked her dress, but it mattered little. She hiked up her skirt a few inches higher and resumed her search for Colton Danfield.

She raced along the fence line that separated the pasture from the cornfield but didn't see either of the men. Stopping to catch her breath, she sent a plea heavenward.

"Lord, I know it's just a sheep, but she's in trouble, and I'm afraid she might die. Please show me where Colton is." When she'd begun thinking of him as Colton instead of Mr. Danfield, she couldn't say. She pushed the thought aside and pressed on.

Beyond the acres of corn, a small orchard perched on a hillside. She shaded her eyes and squinted. Colton's helper, the black man, worked among the trees, his back to her.

She ran toward him, too breathless to call out. As she approached, she realized he was shirtless and she hesitated, but urgency won out over propriety. Holding her skirt to avoid another spill, she hastened through the orchard. Just as she opened her mouth to call to the man, her gaze fell on his bare back. Ugly jagged scars crisscrossed his back. A wave of nausea threatened, but she ordered her stomach to be still and forced her eyes upward to the back of his head where white hairs curled tightly with black ones.

"Sir...could you please...come help..."

The black man spun around, his eyes widening when he caught sight of her. He glanced from side to side and took several strides to an adjacent tree. Snatching his shirt from a low-hanging branch, he shoved his arms in the sleeves and pulled the garment around him. He lowered his eyes.

"Miz Covington. I's sho' sorry. Didn' mean no disrespec'."

She shook her head and gulped air. Pointing behind her, she panted. "One of the sheep. I think it's sick. It's lying in the grass, kicking.... The poor thing needs help."

"What's going on?"

Auralie turned. Colton Danfield approached from the opposite side of the orchard. Alarm filled his eyes when he met her gaze.

"Miss Covington. Are you all right? Is something wrong at the Hancock place?"

She held up her hand, her respirations still coming in short gasps. "You said I could come and get a closer look at the lambs." She paused to breathe. "I was walking through the pasture and one of the sheep is down. I think it's sick or hurt. It sounds like it's in pain."

He lengthened his stride. "Where?"

She pointed. "Up past the top of that farthest slope. It's lying in the grass, groaning."

He exchanged glances with the black man. "Probably one of the ewes." He returned his gaze to her. "Most of the sheep can—" His face grew scarlet. "They don't normally need help— That is, when it's time for them to—" He sent a pleading look back to his helper who simply pressed his lips together.

"Please, come." She hoped the insistence in her tone compelled him. "I'm afraid the poor thing is dying." Her voice broke and Colton winced.

"All right. Show me."

She clutched her skirts tightly so she'd not embarrass herself by falling on her face again. He took her arm and helped her up the inclines and over the rough terrain. A fleeting thought whisked through her mind that she might enjoy his chivalry had it not been for the urgency of the situation.

As they approached the spot where the sheep lay struggling, the black-and-white dog barked furiously.

"Hush up, Free."

Free? An odd name for a dog.

She stood back a pace or two, twisting her ring, as he

knelt by the sheep. He ran his hands over the wooly body and looked up. "It's as I suspected. She's in labor."

"You mean, she's going to—she's having—"

The sheep let out a groan and sharp bleat. Dizziness invaded Auralie's senses, and she feared her knees might buckle.

Colton examined the animal more closely, carefully probing the underbelly. "Well, you were right. She's in trouble. I need your help."

Auralie blanched. Surely he didn't intend for her to— "Do you want me to go back and get—"

"There's no time. Come here and help me." He sent her an imploring look. "Please."

Colton tramped back up the slope with his bandana soaked in water from the tiny rivulet at the bottom of the hill. Auralie sat in the shade of the oak tree, her hem—soiled with grass stains and rumpled from kneeling next to the sheep—primly arranged over her ankles, watching the new mother and her twins get acquainted.

He couldn't stop the grin from spreading across his face and tucked the memory of their shared experience into a secret place in his heart where he kept those treasures he never wanted to forget.

The twin lambs struggled to their feet and bumped against their mother until they found their dinner. Pure exhilaration glowed on Auralie's face as she watched.

She'd paled at first when he directed her to hold the ewe, but fascination soon replaced the panicked look, and awe filled her expression as she helped Colton with the birth.

He walked over and lowered himself to the ground beside her and handed her the wet rag. She cleaned her hands then angled her head to look at Colton. "They're so beautiful. What a miraculous thing to watch. It was so...so..."

He grinned at her. "I'm just glad you didn't swoon."

"Oh." She jerked her head to face him. "Me, too. Look what I would have missed."

He tossed his head back and laughed. He remembered wondering what it might feel like to laugh with Auralie Covington. He wasn't disappointed, and knew at that moment he was losing his heart to her.

Auralie plucked a few clover and dandelion blossoms and gathered them into a small bouquet. "Have you lived here long?"

"Just over five years." Colton relaxed against the trunk of the oak. "When Pastor Winslow retired, he bought this homestead. He'd spent forty-five years in the ministry— thirty of those years as a circuit-riding preacher. He performed my parents' wedding ceremony.

"He was up in years, and before long his health began to fail. I came over from Tucker's Gap—that's where my parents live—and stayed with him, helping him around the place." Colton smiled. "He used to say I was the grandson he never had." His smile faded. "When he went home to be with the Lord, he left this place to me."

Auralie shifted her position and tugged her hem discreetly over her ankles. "I don't remember him." She shrugged. "But then, my family doesn't attend church. The only time I ever went to church was when I visited Belle and her family."

How sad, to have to visit relatives in order to attend worship services. But Colton kept his musing to himself. "Do you visit your cousin often? I don't recall seeing you at the Hancock place before."

She shook her head. "I was away at school when Belle married Lloyd and moved here. I begged to come and visit her, but my father never allowed it until now."

Colton found this puzzling. "But you indicated at dinner last Sunday that the two of you had grown up together."

"Well." She cocked her head as if trying to figure out how to explain. "We didn't really grow up *together*. Belle's family lives south of Athens, so we only got to see each other two or three times a year. Belle is three years older than me, but we got along very well, even when we were young. When I was twelve, my father sent me away to boarding school because he said I needed to make appropriate friends."

Colton studied her dark brown eyes. "He didn't consider your cousin appropriate?"

A tiny frown creased her brow, and she appeared to be studying blades of grass. Her voice took on a pensive tone. "Not my cousin. He didn't like me spending time with the slave children. Of course, he especially didn't like it when he found out I was teaching them to read."

So, what Barnabas told him was true. "I see." He reached over and plucked a dandelion and added it to her diminutive bouquet. "Barnabas told me he remembers you."

She raised her eyes to meet his. "Barnabas?"

"The man who works with me."

Her gaze skittered in the direction of the orchard. "How does he know me?"

"He was a field slave on your father's plantation for more than fifteen years. He said he remembers seeing you coming to the slave quarters and playing with the children."

She stared off at the distant apple trees, fixing her focus on something unseen. Colton could almost hear the thoughts turning over in her mind. When she spoke again, her voice was low and strangled.

"He—Barnabas—was one of my father's field slaves?" She turned to look at him, and her eyes held a stricken look, as if some horrible vision had just been revealed to her. She shuddered visibly.

"Yes." Colton kept his tone gentle. "I bought Barnabas from your father."

She slipped her hand up and touched her trembling fingers to her lips. Tears glistened in her eyes, and an invisible fist punched Colton in the gut. He was about to apologize for upsetting her, but he couldn't imagine what he'd said to evoke such a response. Before he could say a word, she spoke first.

"And you gave him his freedom."

Colton nodded. What kind of cad was he, to make this sweet young lady cry?

Auralie dropped her hand to her midsection and her brow furrowed. "Oh mercy." The words came out as a whisper as if speaking them in a prayer. She turned her eyes back to Colton. "When I came looking for you to tell you the sheep needed help, I saw Barnabas working. He'd…he'd taken his shirt off, and—"

Understanding dawned. "You saw his scars."

She gave a slight nod and dashed away the tears. "I admire you for what you did, giving Barnabas his freedom."

Colton glanced off to the side, emotion welling up within his chest. "He carries papers with him, indicating he is indentured to me, but that's just to prevent a bounty hunter from taking him." He returned his gaze to her. "Barnabas is free to go whenever he wants, and I wrote a statement on those papers saying exactly that. He chooses to stay."

She clasped her hands around her knees. "It must be a glorious thing to be able to take those papers out any time he wants to and read for himself that he is free."

Colton wasn't sure why, but Auralie's statement sent shafts of guilt needling through him. It had never occurred to him to ask Barnabas if he wanted to learn to read. He had all he could handle worrying about some unscrupulous bounty hunter coming by the place when Barnabas was alone and taking him, papers or no papers.

When he didn't answer her, she turned to him with a quizzical arch to her eyebrows. "Can Barnabas read?"

Colton pictured a courageous twelve-year-old girl sneaking off to the slave quarters to teach little colored children to read, and shame leached into his heart. "No. He can't."

Her lips parted in disbelief. "Why didn't you ever teach him to read?"

He hunched his shoulders. "I don't know. It never occurred to me." The moment the words fell out of his mouth, he regretted them. A little thing like breaking the law hadn't mattered to her at the age of twelve. With Barnabas a free man, what prevented him from teaching his friend to read?

Chapter 12

Auralie bit her lip and waited for Mr. Danfield to growl at her, pointing out that how he chose to handle his hired help was none of her business. When would she ever learn to think before she spoke? Sure enough, a frown carved a furrow in his brow, but instead of bellowing his indignation at her comment, he nodded slowly.

"You're right. I'll ask Barnabas if he'd like to learn to read." A small sheepish grin tilted his mouth at a lopsided angle. "After all, if you can teach a bunch of children to read when you were just a kid yourself, I can teach one man."

She gulped. "I'm so sorry. I don't know what comes over me sometimes. It was entirely unfitting of me to ask such a question. My father constantly berates me for stepping out of place. Please forgive me, Mr. Danfield."

A smile stretched across his face. He reached out his hand and covered hers, halting the twisting of her ring she hadn't been aware she was doing. "There's nothing to forgive. I'm glad you pointed out the opportunity to teach Barnabas to read." He gave her hand a brief squeeze before releasing it. The pressure of his fingers sent tingles up her arm, and she stifled a soft gasp. He must have felt it, too, because his eyes widened, and he glanced down at their hands the instant they parted.

Warmth stole into her cheeks. She knew she should tell him about her betrothal, but the familiar ache that pinched her stomach every time she thought about the coming marriage swelled, and she swallowed back the words.

He must have mistaken her reaction for embarrassment over her impulsive statement.

"Really, I'm not angry at you. You opened my eyes and made me see I'd neglected something very important. I should thank you."

She'd never heard a man say such a thing. All her life, she'd witnessed men assert themselves and manipulate others, bluster their authority and wield control like a weapon. Over the years, she'd learned to lower her eyes in submission and shrink into the background to make herself as invisible as possible, quietly excusing herself and tiptoeing away the moment the opportunity presented itself. But Mr. Danfield's gentle tone unnerved her. All the elocution lessons and deportment exercises she'd endured with Miss Josephine Westbrook at the Rose Hill Female Academy did not equip her with a ready reply to his unexpected response.

"Mr. Danfield, I...I..."

His expression turned solicitous. "Have I upset you in some way? Because that was not my intention."

Wonderment filled her. "You didn't upset me. I didn't expect—that is, I'd assumed all men—" She stopped herself before saying something sure to insult him, but he finished her thought.

"You thought all men were like your father?"

Was she that transparent? Oddly, the idea didn't frighten her, at least not with Mr. Danfield. She relaxed her shoulders and nodded. "Yes, I suppose I do."

He sat forward and rested his arms on his upraised knees. "Pastor Winslow taught me a great deal, and he always seemed to use common, everyday things as object lessons." A twinkle lit his eyes. "Around here, that usually involves sheep."

She couldn't help but smile and raised her eyes to watch the newborn lambs again.

After a moment, he continued. "You've probably heard the parable in the Bible about the shepherd who left the ninety-nine sheep to go out and find the one that was lost. Of course, that parable is meant to illustrate how we should seek people who need the Lord, but Pastor Winslow used it to draw a different picture. What kind of man was the shepherd?"

She cocked her head and pondered the question. "I suppose he was diligent about his job."

Mr. Danfield smiled and nodded. "Yes, he was that. But what made him diligent?"

Auralie turned her gaze back to the twin lambs tottering unsteadily next to their mother. Who wouldn't want to diligently protect something so vulnerable and helpless? She lifted her shoulders. "My father would say the sheep were worth money so diligence ensured a better profit. But I presume the shepherd had a different reason."

Mr. Danfield's rich, deep-throated laugh made her heart skip, and she hoped he'd laugh again.

"The shepherd *cared* about the sheep, and he demonstrated his compassion by showing that even the least of them was just as important as the rest. Pastor Winslow used to say every one of his sheep was important, just like every one of God's children is important." He pointed to the new mother and her babies. "When you found this ewe in distress, you could have just left her to fend for herself. After all, even if she had died, there's still a whole flock of sheep down the hill."

Auralie gave a soft gasp. "I couldn't do that. Look at her. Look at those little ones. How could anyone just leave her to die?"

"Exactly my point." When she turned to look at him, he was smiling at her. "Pastor Winslow emphasized that if Jesus died for the sins of all of us, then He views every person the same way the shepherd does his sheep. The pastor's point was that we shouldn't treat some people better or worse than others because we assign them a different level of importance. It was a valuable lesson that I hope I never forget."

"Your Pastor Winslow sounds like an extraordinary man." *And so are you, Colton Danfield.* She pressed her lips together before the words found their way past her tongue. "I must say this has been a very enlightening morning, but I fear it's well past the noon hour. Belle and Mammy will be sending out a search party if I don't get back."

Mr. Danfield pushed away from the tree trunk and stood. He reached down and grasped both her hands and helped her to her feet. For a moment—an eternity—they stood facing each other with joined hands. His warm eyes and devastating smile robbed her of speech.

He released her hands and took a step backward. "May I see you home?"

At the moment, she couldn't think of anything she'd like better. She nodded and took one last look at the lambs she'd helped usher into the world. "Will they be all right?"

"Oh sure." He gave a sharp whistle. "Free will look after them." The dog came bounding up the hill, and Mr. Danfield gave him a pat. "You have two new babies to take care of, fella."

"I don't think I've ever heard of a dog named Free."

"Barnabas named him."

She smiled. No other explanation was needed.

As they approached the boundary line between the two properties, Mr. Danfield cleared his throat. "Would you be offended if I asked you to call me Colton?"

Her breath caught. *You're engaged. Tell him.* Her heart and her common sense waged war. Until it was announced, the engagement wasn't official. At least that's what she kept telling herself.

At some point, she'd already begun thinking of him as Colton, and she couldn't deny how the silent utterance of his name in her private thoughts set an entire flock of hummingbirds loose in her stomach.

"I find nothing offensive in calling you by your given name, but you must call me Auralie."

"Auralie."

She had to remind herself to breathe at the sound of her own name. The way he said it was melodic, as if the wind whispered. Her heart pounded so hard, the impact vibrated throughout her body.

What was it Belle had told her? *"All I'm trying to do is make you visualize how it could be if you were to do your own choosing."*

The grass was still wet with morning dew as Colton made his way to the pasture to check on the newest lambs. Free met him with tail wagging, as if proudly showing off *his* new babies. Only three days old, the twins stuck close to their mother, but they looked stronger than they had the morning they struggled into the world. For the hundredth time, the memory of Auralie kneeling in the grass, holding the ewe's head and crooning quietly to calm the nervous mother, slid easily into his thoughts. Who would have thought the daughter of Shelby Covington would exhibit such tender compassion? Chagrin pricked him when he remembered how he judged her—assumed she'd be spoiled and arrogant by virtue of her lineage. He was happy to be wrong.

He'd never stopped to think how a woman like Auralie lived under a cloud of intimidation, but that's exactly what she'd implied. Did Covington really bully his own daughter into submission? The idea rankled Colton more than he cared to admit.

What are you doing, Danfield? He shook his head. Time after time he warned himself against allowing feelings for Auralie to take root, and every time the feelings won out. Hadn't he pushed away the budding attraction? Didn't he try to discipline his thoughts?

"Hmph. If I did, I wasn't very successful." He reprimanded himself all the way back to the barn, but blocking Auralie from his thoughts was an exercise he found impossible. He'd exchanged a few glances and smiles with her at church yesterday—each time setting his heart to thumping like a schoolboy's. At the end of the service, Jack McCaffey snagged him to discuss some information regarding Shelby Covington's pledge to bring the railroad into their area. By the time he broke away from Jack, the Hancock carriage was leaving the churchyard.

No good could come of seeking more than friendship with her. With a heavy sigh, he grabbed a hoe from the barn and headed for the cornfield.

The sun slipped behind a cloud, and the air held the scent of rain. He began swinging his hoe at the intruding weeds, hoping to get several rows done before the skies opened

up. Hard work. That's what he needed. Nothing like aching
muscles and sweat to take a man's mind off…

In the distance, a stylish gray carriage pulled up at the
Hancocks' front door. Colton straightened and squinted.
Mrs. Hancock's servant, Sam, loaded bags behind the driver's seat. Auralie came out onto the porch, tying her bonnet under her chin. Mrs. Hancock followed. They hugged,
and then Auralie turned toward Colton's farm and paused.
He couldn't tell from the distance whether or not she saw
him. A minute later, she and Mammy stepped into the carriage and drove off, leaving Mrs. Hancock standing and
waving from the porch.

Colton leaned on his hoe and watched the carriage dis-
appear beyond the trees. She'd not mentioned her visit was
growing short, not that it was any of his business.

"Just as well," he muttered, but his words rang hollow.

Colton dragged his sleeve across his forehead. His back
and shoulders ached and sweat dripped from his hair, but
taking out his frustrations on the weeds was better than
brooding. When he got to the end of the row, he picked up
the canteen looped over the fence post and took a drink.
As he returned the canteen to the post, he caught sight of
three men beyond his property line.

He instantly turned to ascertain Barnabas's whereabouts
and found him working on fence posts near the barn. Colton
returned his focus to the trio who now studied an unrolled
scroll.

His surly mood kicked a notch higher. He intended to
find out once and for all who these men were and what
they were doing so close to his land. He strode to the edge
of the cornfield toward the men. If grumpiness hadn't already taken up residence within him, he might be tempted
to laugh. The men, dressed in fine suits, brocade vests with

glittering watch chains, and silk cravats, looked as out of place tramping around through the underbrush as a mule in church. Engrossed in whatever the paper in their hands contained, they didn't look up until Colton called to them.

"Good afternoon, gentlemen."

The three jerked their heads up in unison. Colton stopped at the edge of his property, and one of the men walked toward him. His thick reddish brown hair and square jaw gave him an air of nobility, and Colton wondered if this was the same man Barnabas saw.

"May I ask what you're doing out here?"

The man lifted his chin and sent a sweeping glance down Colton's dirty work clothes and muddy boots. "Are you Danfield?"

"That's right." He held out his hand.

The man gave Colton's hand a brief shake. "My name is Covington." The man's haughty demeanor hung in the air like a stench from mucking out the stalls. Covington paused momentarily, as if waiting for Colton to react to the name. When Colton remained stonefaced, Covington continued. "My men and I are conducting a geographical survey, marking boundary lines for a client—an old family friend."

The hackles on the back of Colton's neck rose, and his spine stiffened. Covington's disdain didn't bother him nearly as much as what he didn't say, but Colton didn't intend to let Covington walk away without confronting him with what he knew.

"A friend of mine witnessed you several days ago, taking survey measurements across my land. I'd like to know why."

A sneer pulled one side of Covington's mouth upward. "*Your* land? Can a man who doesn't have the means to purchase land truly be called a landowner?"

Every shred of self-control Colton possessed prevented him from planting a fist on the side of Covington's aristocratic jaw. "If you'll check the record books in the land office and the tax assessor's office, you'll find I am the legal owner of this piece of property."

"Through another man's benevolence." Covington sniffed. He reached into his inside coat pocket and pulled out a small, leather-bound notebook with gold filigree stamped on the front. He flipped a few pages. "The previous owner was an old man by the name of Winslow, and he left it to you when he died."

Colton clamped his teeth and pursed his lips, determined not to allow the man to detect any inkling of agitation at the disrespectful reference to his dear friend and mentor, or his implied insult. "That is true. Does inheritance make me any less the rightful owner of the property?"

"Legally, no. At least for now."

Colton ached to grab this arrogant snob and bloody his nose, but if he landed in jail, what might happen to Barnabas?

"You didn't answer my question."

Covington tucked the notebook back into his coat pocket. "What question was that?"

Colton spread his feet and crossed his arms. "Why were you surveying across my land?"

The same insolent smirk appeared. "We were using the southeast corner of the little shanty there as a benchmark for locating the corner of the property."

No point in inviting more ridicule by informing Covington that little shanty was his home. Besides, Colton was quite certain all the condescending talk was a smoke screen. If Covington thought he could rile Colton to the point where his anger would make him take leave of his common sense, he might miss what was really going on. The first chance he got, he planned to go to town and make some inquiries with Randall Kimber at the land office. If there was anything underhanded brewing, Colton wanted to find out.

Colton uncrossed his arms and planted his hands on his hips. "I have to get back to work."

Covington snorted. "Of course you do." He turned to walk away, but Colton stopped him.

"Mr. Covington."

The man halted and turned, his forehead furrowed in patronizing disdain. "Yes?"

"A thought just occurred to me. Do you suppose your father is going to live forever?"

Covington's brows dipped. "What?"

Amusement tickled Colton's belly, but he held it in. "Unless your father lives forever, you're going to inherit Covington Plantation some day. How nice that you will become a real landowner through another man's benevolence."

Colton turned and strode back to the cornfield.

Chapter 13

Auralie forced her attention back to the discussion of tea cakes, tarts, and petit fours. Gabrielle Bolden held court in the parlor at Covington Plantation, instructing Auralie on the proper arrangement of the buffet table for tea. The woman destined to be Auralie's mother-in-law arrived armed with lists, schedules, menus, and decoration plans, complete with instructions for Auralie and her mother.

"You do understand, of course, each menu item has been selected with utmost thought and consideration for color, shape, and texture, as well as taste."

"Forgive my confusion, Mrs. Bolden." Auralie intertwined her fingers in her lap, twisting her ring. She curled her toes inside her slippers at the disapproving frown from her mother, who sat across the room. "I was under the impression the engagement party would be held in the evening. I don't understand the need for planning an afternoon tea."

Mrs. Bolden raised one eyebrow. "There will be very important people coming from as far as Atlanta and Augusta—senators and their wives, diplomats, and various dignitaries. Some will arrive in the afternoon, and we must be prepared to serve them refreshments befitting their station."

Auralie wilted under the scrutinizing glare of the woman's green eyes. She didn't care a fig about planning this soiree, but her mother did. As she expected, an indignant cough came from across the room.

"Auralie received the guest list from your son and has spent a great deal of time in preparation for the announcement party."

Auralie's eyes widened. How could her mother speak such an exaggeration? "Mother, I—"

The elder Covington woman merely gave a nearly imperceptible shake of her head to Auralie. "We're quite prepared to entertain the most elite of those listed and will take every pain necessary to ensure a most triumphant event, surpassed only by the wedding itself."

Mrs. Bolden pressed her lips together in an artificial and condescending smile. "Of course."

Auralie wasn't fooled. Gabrielle Bolden intended to dictate every detail of the event.

Phoebe Covington refused to be outdone. "I've commissioned ten ivory tablecloths of the finest Irish linen, to be overlaid with Belgian lace. In addition, I've ordered twelve dozen napkins in a coordinating brocade." She finished with a slight bob of her head, no doubt intended to put an exclamation point on her announcement.

Mrs. Bolden advised that the etched stemware she'd ordered from Boston should arrive any day. Auralie's mother described the finest of silver and crystal candelabras she'd chosen for the serving table. The duet of egos made Auralie dizzy, and she longed to be back in the sheep meadow with Colton, watching the lambs. She stiffened her jaw against the yawn that threatened to expose her boredom.

Auralie's mother tugged at her cuff and sat forward in her chair. "Mrs. Bolden, our cook makes an excellent pecan shortbread that is particularly nice with tea."

Mrs. Bolden fluttered her hand in a dismissive motion and uttered an airy titter. "Oh my dear Mrs. Covington, we will bring in the best chefs and pastry artists from Savannah and Charleston. Surely you didn't think to entrust such an important occasion to your servants." She pressed a lace-gloved hand to her bosom and shook her head. None of her precise curls dared to slip out of place.

Auralie's stomach rolled over. Is this what her life was destined to be?

"So, let us summarize what we have thus far." Mrs. Bolden perched a pair of bejeweled eyeglasses on the bridge of her nose and looked over the sheet of stationery in front of her on which she'd written several lists.

"For the tea, we shall serve Darjeeling, orange pekoe, ginger spice tea, and a delightful oolong tea I sampled the last time I was in Richmond." She jotted down a notation, and then sent an evaluating glance around the room. "This room might do for the tea. If the weather is nice, we'll leave those French doors open to the veranda. That way the space might not seem so cramped."

Auralie gulped. Cramped? If the cavernous room was any larger, it would echo. She slid her gaze to the window and wondered for the twentieth time that day what Colton was doing, and whether or not he knew she'd left Belle's.

"Miss Auralie, you mustn't daydream." Mrs. Bolden's voice, while veiled with overtones of refinement, grated on Auralie's ears. "My son will expect his wife to be attuned to his needs and be capable of engaging in intelligent conversation. You can hardly do that while staring out the window."

"Yes ma'am." Auralie itched to have this ordeal over. A quick glance showed Mother's displeasure at her daughter's lack of attention. A knot twisted in Auralie's stomach.

Lord, I'm not giving up praying and asking You to please put a stop to this marriage. I love You, Lord. Help me trust You with this.

She tried to relax her stomach muscles that had begun to cramp. Mrs. Bolden went down her list of delicacies for the afternoon tea.

"Finger sandwiches of cucumber, watercress, liver pâté, and veal pâté. As accompaniments to the sandwiches, tomato aspic, cranberry apple press, and ambrosia will be offered." She checked off the items as she announced them. "We must have at least four different kinds of tarts, equally pleasing to the eye as to the palate. With that in mind, I've chosen red current tarts, lemon chess tarts, marmalade tarts, and ginger buttermilk tarts." She glanced up at Auralie and her mother, as if daring them to challenge any of her choices.

"An exquisite variety." Her mother's stiff smile appeared ready to crack. "They will make an interesting arrangement on the platters."

Auralie's back ached from sitting in such a stiff position, but she dared not move and draw attention to herself.

Mrs. Bolden gave a single nod and turned a page. "I've selected the following pastries: Bavarian cream, chocolate liqueur, brandied apricot, and sherried fig. Of course the finest spiced tea cakes and petit fours will be a necessity." She released a sigh, as if she'd spent the entire morning in the kitchen creating the delectable tidbits listed on her paper.

"Mrs. Bolden, I don't mean to be disagreeable, but none

of us are certain when Perry will arrive back on American shores." Auralie swallowed back a spoonful of guilt at her fib. Disagreeing was exactly what she wished to do. "Hadn't we ought to wait until he is home before making such lavish plans?"

A tiny frown tilted Gabrielle Bolden's brow into a V. "The last communication we had from Perry indicated he was sailing on the twenty-fifth of April. Allowing approximately six weeks for the trans-Atlantic voyage, and barring adverse weather, he should arrive within the next two weeks."

"I see." Invisible fingers clutched Auralie's throat. "The letter I received was water stained and the date of his departure was blurred." Two weeks. She envisioned a prisoner counting off the days until his execution.

Dear God, please intervene. The time is growing so short. I beg You to free me from this marriage.

Mrs. Bolden cleared her throat, her annoyance clearly visible. "Now let us discuss the menu for the ball."

The woman droned on for the next hour, introducing an extensive list of rich and impressive foods. By the time their meeting was concluded, Auralie didn't care if she ever saw food again. But she still had to endure a luncheon with both her mother and future mother-in-law. She managed to swallow a few bites but longed to be back on Belle's side porch, listening to her cousin tease and laugh and watching the lambs frolic in the distant pasture.

While her mother and Mrs. Bolden retired to the conservatory, Auralie slipped upstairs to her room. Exhaustion overwhelmed her and she collapsed on the bed. Within minutes, Mammy tapped on her door and came bustling over to the bed.

"Let me he'p you get that gown off so's you can take a nap. You look worn to a frazzle."

As Mammy unfastened the garment, the starch Auralie employed to get her through the hours spent with Mrs. Bolden and her mother evaporated, and she melted into tears. "Mammy, it's awful. If I have to spend another day with that woman, I'll lose whatever sanity I have left." She whirled around to face her dear old friend. "What if Perry is just like her? What if he's worse?" She covered her face with her hands. "I can't do this."

Mammy slipped the gown and crinolines off. "There, there, honey girl. Did yo' fo'get we's prayin'? We beggin' God fo' His mercy, and He hear us. Now you come ovah here and rest, while ole Mammy sit right here in dis chair beside you."

Auralie curled into a ball on the bed while Mammy covered her with a light sheet. "There is one good thing. Father was called away on business at the last minute, so I didn't have to face his inquisition."

"I don' know what dat is, but it don' sound good."

Auralie propped her head up with one hand. "Mammy, I want to go back to Belle's house."

A smile twitched around Mammy's lips. "Did you tell yo' mama that Miss Belle be in da family way?"

"No! And don't you say anything. Mother would never allow me to go back if she knew Belle was expecting. She wouldn't think it proper because I'm yet unmarried." She snuffled a giggle.

Mammy angled her head and plopped one fist on her ample hip. "What be ticklin' yo' funny bone?"

Perhaps it was the depth of her exhaustion, but she suddenly couldn't stop laughing. Gales of mirth brought tears to her eyes, and she pressed her hands to her stomach and held her midsection. "Oh my goodness…" She wiped her eyes. "When Mother asked about my activities while I was visiting Belle, I had to bite my lip to keep from giggling.

Can't you see the expression on Mother's face if she knew I'd carried lemonade to Colton and Barnabas, had Sunday dinner with a farmer, helped in the birthing of two lambs, and sat in the meadow grass under a tree getting to know Colton?" She burst into laughter again. "She'd swoon."

Mammy's shoulders shook silently and a broad smile split her face. "Honey girl, I jus' loves hearin' you laugh."

Auralie sat up and reached for Mammy's hand. "I want to go back. As soon as Mrs. Bolden leaves, I want to go back to Belle's."

Auralie begged to be excused from the discussion of flower arrangements, candelabras, and string quartets, claiming a headache. It wasn't a lie. Her head hadn't stopped throbbing from the moment Gabrielle Bolden stepped through the front door. Thank goodness the woman was leaving in the morning.

A late afternoon breeze wafted through the double doors leading to the small private balcony off Auralie's bedroom. How many times had she stood out there as a girl, attempting to see past the oaks and pines to the slave quarters hidden beyond the rise behind the stables. Where were those children now—the ones she'd taught to read? Were they still working at Covington Plantation? Had they been sold? Were they still alive?

A shudder rippled through her as she recalled the ghastly scars on Barnabas's back. She turned away from the balcony and tried to banish the unspeakable picture from her thoughts. Instead, she welcomed the image of Colton and his sheep. She reclined on the velvet-covered chaise and let her eyes drift closed. Colton's lopsided grin and the newborn lambs eased into her musings. A thrill danced through her stomach when she remembered his hand over hers.

The urgency of the mother sheep's dilemma and the exhilaration of witnessing the births had taken center stage that day. Afterward, as they'd sat beneath the oak and talked, she didn't think to tell Colton she'd been bidden to return home in a few days. She knew it was presumptuous to think he'd care whether she stayed or left, but she wanted to *think* he cared. When the carriage had arrived from Covington Plantation two mornings ago, she remembered pausing to look across the meadow toward Colton's place. She'd seen him in the cornfield, but the distance prevented her from seeing his face. She wished now she'd told him good-bye.

She shook her head and opened her eyes. "I must stop this. God, unless You act in a miraculous way, I'm going to spend the rest of my life with Perry, not Colton."

She swung her feet off the side of the chaise and sat up. Colton's deep-throated laughter lingered in her mind, as did his promise to ask Barnabas if he wanted to learn to read. Her heart smiled imagining the stirring of realization in Barnabas's eyes when he read his first word. Oh, how she'd love to be there to witness it.

An idea dawned. Of course, why hadn't she thought of it before?

She rose and crossed to her bedroom door, cracking it open. She peeked out and listened. Her mother and Mrs. Bolden must still be trying to outdo each other over the plans to decorate the ballroom for the upcoming festivities. She tiptoed into the hall and headed toward the attic staircase and the wonderland of adventure hidden away on the third floor. She'd spent countless days up there as a child, exploring and playing games of imagination.

One of the steps creaked beneath her foot. She froze and held her breath, listening. A snicker wiggled its way up her throat when she recalled the times she and Belle spent childhood days creeping through the attic, hoping to avoid detection by the adults. No one came to investigate, so she climbed up the steep, narrow staircase to the white-washed, chipped door.

The attic appeared much smaller than she remembered, and much more cluttered. Sunlight fell in through two small windows. Sheet-covered furniture created ghostly forms, stacks of crates sat haphazardly arranged, and several rolled up carpets leaned against one wall. But the item for which she searched was nowhere in sight. As quietly as possible, she moved crates and pushed a chair to one side, stirring dust motes that floated in the light streaming from the window, like tiny fairies dancing on sunbeams.

A small chest with a broken latch sat beneath the window. Inside she found dresses she'd worn when she was a child. A tug of remembrance caused her to pick them up and finger the cloth. They weren't fancy. No ribbons or special stitching, no pearl buttons or satin sashes adorned them. They were the simple dresses she'd worn to play. She sorted through the pile.

And she remembered.

A spark of anger kindled within her. "These are the dresses I took to the slave children. I remember giving these to the little girls when I sneaked down there with a basket of cookies and fruit. How did they get up here in the attic?" There was only one way, and it grieved her to think her father had ordered the little slave girls to give back the dresses she'd outgrown and had given to them. She tucked them back into the chest and closed it, sadness gripping her heart.

The dancing fairies tickled her nose, and she pinched her nostrils shut to ward off a sneeze. A tapestry lay across an unwieldy lump. Auralie moved a birdcage and an old dress form and pulled back the tapestry to find the object of her search—an old leather-bound trunk where her childhood storybooks were packed.

The hinges squeaked when she lifted the lid. She paused and glanced over her shoulder. No footsteps sounded on the stairs—no voice challenged her right to be in the attic. Her hands rummaged through the trunk, extracting volumes to hold up to the light so she could read their titles. Finally her fingers found the one for which she searched.

"McGuffey's Second Eclectic Reader." A smile warmed her all the way to her toes. The same book she'd used to teach the slave children to read would unlock a whole new world for Barnabas as well. She closed the trunk lid and replaced the tapestry and other items. Slipping the book within the folds of her skirt, she sneaked back down the stairs to her room.

Chapter 14

Auralie removed her bonnet. "It's only been a week, but it feels like I've been gone for a year."

Belle's merry laugh was balm to her soul, and she pulled her cousin into a hug.

"Sam is taking your bags up to your room, and I asked him to open the windows in there as well." Belle squeezed Auralie again. "Oh, it's so good to have you home." She giggled. "I meant it's so good to have you back."

"I knew what you meant." Auralie cocked her head. "Being here feels like what *home* is supposed to mean." She looped her arm through Belle's, and they headed for their favorite wicker chairs on the side porch. "Have you heard any more from Lloyd?"

Belle regaled her with all the details of Lloyd's last letter. "He said he might come home by the end of June, but only for a couple of weeks."

"Have you told him yet?" A warm flush filled Auralie's face. "That you're…"

Belle shook her head. "Some things you just can't put in a letter. But I did write that I had a special surprise for him when he returned home." She sighed. "I could barely contain myself when I answered his last letter. I'm just aching to tell him. He's going to be a wonderful father."

Maizie stepped out onto the porch with a tray and set it down on the small table between the two chairs. "I made some fresh lemonade, 'cause I know it yo' fav'rite, Miss Auralie. An' dem cookies be Miss Belle's fav'rite snickerdoodles." She leaned toward Auralie. "It be real good to have you back. You make Miss Belle smile." The black woman grinned and bustled back to the summer kitchen.

"Poor Maizie. I'm afraid I've been rather grumpy." Belle nibbled on a cinnamon-encrusted cookie. "Does Mr. Danfield know you're back?"

Auralie paused with her frosty glass of lemonade halfway to her lips. She could attempt to pull a veil over Belle's eyes, but her cousin knew her well. "I doubt it. He's much too busy with his farm and his sheep to care one way or the other anyway." She took a long sip of lemonade and allowed herself to hope she was wrong.

Belle arched her eyebrows. "It might interest you to know that he stopped by here two days ago."

"He did?" Auralie's heart turned over, and she knew the spark in her voice betrayed her.

Belle munched on another cookie. "I'm so hungry these days. Maizie says I'm eating for two, so I'm supposed to be hungry."

Auralie waited.

Belle patted her lips with a napkin. "Remind me later to show you the little gown I finished for the baby while you were gone. It's so tiny, but Maizie assures me it's plenty large enough for a newborn. I embroidered a delicate design in yellow around the neck, and the stitches—"

"Belle?"

"Hmm?"

"Are you going to tell me why Colton…uh, Mr. Danfield stopped by?"

The twinkle in her cousin's eyes belied her innocent expression. "Oh, I thought you were much too busy to care one way or the other."

"*Belle*…I said *he* was probably much too busy. Now are you going to tell me or am I going to confiscate the rest of those cookies?"

Giggles bubbled from Belle's throat, and she leaned forward as if divulging a great secret. "When I saw him walking across the meadow, I met him on the front porch. He seemed…kind of lost. He mumbled something about lambs, and then he asked if I'd heard from you. I said no, and he just stood there like he didn't know what else to say." She pressed her hand to her chest. "It was so romantic."

Romantic? Auralie couldn't see Belle's reasoning, but perhaps being in the family way made her take strange notions. "Is that all? I mean, did he say anything else?"

Belle took on a sympathetic expression. "He asked me if I would give you a message the next time I saw you." She sighed and tipped her head to one side.

"And?"

"And what?"

Auralie gritted her teeth. "If you don't tell me what he said, Belle, I swear I'm going to—"

Belle dissolved into a burst of laughter, and Auralie sat there trying to scowl at her cousin. Finally wiping her eyes, Belle fanned herself with her napkin. "He said to tell you the lambs were running and playing. And he said something else—something about keeping his promise."

A thrill swelled in her midsection. He was teaching Barnabas to read. She couldn't contain the joy that fluttered through her. A smile spread across her face.

"Well?"

Auralie glanced at Belle. "Well, what?"

Belle crossed her arms over her chest in mock indignation. "Are you going to tell me what this promise is that he's keeping?"

A song took wing in Auralie's heart, but this was not something she could share.

"No."

Belle pretended to sulk, but Auralie knew her cousin wasn't truly miffed, especially when she gave Auralie a hug and told her she was going to take a nap. Auralie opened her bag and found the McGuffey's reader tucked in between a chemise and a nightgown. After checking to make sure Belle was asleep, she took the book and headed to the summer kitchen where she found Mammy and Maizie singing while they worked.

"Maizie, are there any more of those snickerdoodles left?"

"They sho' is. Miss Belle still hungry?"

"No." Auralie bit her lip and wondered if she should divulge her purpose for asking. "Might I get a dozen or so in a small basket?"

She slid her gaze to Mammy who raised one eyebrow and gave her a knowing look. Maizie fetched a basket and lined it with a checkered napkin, filling it with the spicy confections. All the while, Mammy spoke without saying a word, but her eyes warned Auralie to guard her heart.

"Thank you, Maizie." She glanced back at Mammy. "I won't be long."

It was all she could do to keep from skipping down the

stone walkway. With the McGuffey's tucked under her arm, she set out across the meadow, her focus fixed on the hillside where the sheep grazed. A number of lambs pranced and scampered to and fro, but Auralie couldn't distinguish which ones were the twins she helped birth. The closer she got, the greater the joy in her heart.

She lifted her face to the spring breeze, relishing the feel of freedom. She never realized before how sweet the meadow grass smelled or how soothing the harmony of the birds. What a privilege to drink it in and let it saturate her spirit.

"What are you doing here?"

Auralie jerked her head toward the voice that bellowed across the meadow from the wooded area that bordered Colton's place. Three men, looking entirely out of place in their tailored frock coats and fancy vests, stood in a cluster at the edge of the woods with measuring equipment. One of them was her brother. She halted as he strode toward her, his expression stormy.

"Dale. What are *you* doing here?"

He planted his hands on his hips. "Suppose you answer my question first, little sister."

Her hands grew clammy and her pulse tapped out a staccato beat. "I'm visiting with Cousin Belle." She turned and pointed. "That's her and Lloyd's house."

Dale glowered at her. "I know where our cousin lives, and Father said something about you visiting her while Lloyd is away. But what are you doing *here?*" He gestured around them. "This isn't Lloyd Hancock's land. It belongs to a man named Danfield."

She never realized before how much Dale's voice sounded like their father's. "I'm aware of whose land it is. Mr. Danfield said I could come and watch the lambs whenever I wanted."

A sarcastic smirk tipped one corner of Dale's mouth. "The lambs. I suppose you're bringing cookies to the lambs as well?" He thumped his fingers against her basket.

"I'm merely being neighborly."

Dale crossed his arms across his chest. "Neighborly. Dirt farmers are not our neighbors, Auralie."

"Oh, stop being such a snob, Dale. There is nothing wrong with extending a kindness."

He narrowed his eyes at her. "Do I have to remind you that you're engaged to Perry Bolden?"

Her engagement was the one thing of which she needed no reminding. "The engagement hasn't been formally announced. Besides, I'm not doing anything wrong."

"Auralie, think about what you're doing." He hissed through clenched teeth at her. "The Boldens are very influential and powerful. You're endangering your reputation—and Perry's. What will Perry think when he arrives home and learns you've been consorting with the likes of Danfield? Not to mention Thaddeus Bolden is Father's biggest supporter. He'd be outraged if he knew you were traipsing around seeing another man behind his son's back."

"Oh, for goodness' sake. You make it sound as if I'm committing some horrible sin." Auralie's ire swelled in her stomach. Her purpose in coming back to Belle's was to escape the rigid parameters under which she was forced to conduct herself at Covington Plantation—at least for a time. "How is taking a basket of cookies to a neighbor outrageous?"

"A family of our standing in the state is always under the magnifying glass." He leaned in closer so he was nearly nose to nose with her. "And don't forget the effect any indiscretions of yours could have on my future with Gwendolyn. Our wedding is less than a month away, and I won't take kindly to you creating a scandal."

Auralie's mouth fell open. "A scandal! Dale, what are you accusing me of?"

Dale's hand snaked out and curled around her arm. "Anything you do to create gossip will not only destroy your union with Perry Bolden, it could also ruin Father's chances for winning the election."

She tried to yank her arm away, but Dale held it fast. "I'm not as naive as you think, Dale. I know why I'm being forced into this marriage. Thaddeus Bolden is paying a great deal of money to smooth Father's way to the governor's seat in exchange for political favors." She pulled against Dale's grip again and when she did so, the McGuffey's reader she had tucked under her arm fell at her feet.

Dale bent and snatched it up. "What do you plan to do with this?"

She froze and her mouth refused to work. When she tried to take it back, Dale pulled it out of her reach.

"Up to your old habits? I seem to recall Father sending you away to school to protect the family name the last time you used this book." He glanced over his shoulder toward Colton's place. "Little sister, teaching a slave to read is against the law."

"Barnabas isn't a slave. He's free." The instant she uttered the words, she wished she could snatch them back, but it was too late.

Dale's eyes widened. "Is that so? If that is the case, Danfield is in violation of the law. Any slave owner who frees a slave is expected to see to it he leaves the state."

Embers of anger sparked to life within her. "Barnabas carries papers showing he is indentured to Colton Danfield, not that it's any of your business."

"You best mind your place and do what's expected of you." He shoved the McGuffey's into his pocket. "Father isn't going to be happy about this." He started to stomp away, but she called after him.

"Dale, I'm not anybody's property. Not Father's and not Perry's."

He turned with his arms akimbo. "That sounds like you're declaring your independence."

She tilted her head and considered his challenge. "Maybe I am."

From the doorway of the barn, Colton watched the animated discussion between Auralie and her brother taking place on the far side of the sheep fence. Mixed emotions tugged him in multiple directions. When he'd caught sight of her coming across the meadow with a basket over her arm, his heart leaped in his chest. He'd thought he'd seen the last of her after she climbed into that fancy carriage almost a week ago. Emptiness dogged his steps for days. How he wanted to tell her about the way Barnabas's eyes lit up when Colton asked him if he'd like to learn to read. Just when he'd gotten accustomed to knowing she was close by, running into her at church, watching her laughing at the lambs' antics, she left without so much as a good-bye.

Seeing she'd returned initiated explosions of pure joy churning through him he didn't want to contain. After weeks of sending his heart explicit instructions to keep Auralie Covington at arm's length, exhilaration broke through like a landslide.

A check in his spirit snagged his attention. In tandem with the thrill, gall burned in his chest watching the confrontation between her and her brother. He couldn't hear their words, but their posture and gestures bespoke anger. The only thing that prevented him from charging to Auralie's defense was the certainty that the argument was about him. Auralie was, after all, headed in the direction of the sheep pasture when her brother intercepted her. No doubt Dale Covington considered him unfit company for his sister.

The siblings parted, and the slump of Auralie's shoulders sent an arrow of grief through Colton. She stood looking toward his place, as if trying to decide whether or not to proceed. Finally, she turned and headed back to the Hancock home.

Colton's stomach curled into a knot of frustration. Common sense told him he had no business having feelings for a girl like Auralie. His heart disagreed.

He set aside the ax he'd been repairing and headed to the orchard where Barnabas was pruning some of the apple trees the deer had damaged. His friend waved when he saw him coming.

"We goin' to have a good crop o' apples this year, Mistah Colton, if dem deer don't eat 'em all." Barnabas pulled on one of the limbs pointing out the dozens of buds. "Even better than las' year."

Colton looked over the trees Barnabas had finished. He'd done his usual fine job. But examining Barnabas's work wasn't his reason for hiking down to the orchard. "Those men are back again."

Barnabas craned his neck and looked through the trees. "How many times dey gots to measure?"

Colton swept his gaze around the perimeter of the orchard and down past the pasture where the forested land in question bordered his. "That has me concerned as well. It doesn't generally require a team of three men to make repeated visits over a period of two weeks to determine where the property lines lie. I told you I already had words with Covington and he evaded my question about why they felt the need to take calculations across my land. Something doesn't smell right about this." He slapped Barnabas on the shoulder. "Just…be careful. Keep your eyes and ears open, especially when you're out here working alone."

"Mistah Colton, you know I always carry my paper wi' me." He patted his shirt pocket. "God be takin' care o' me, so don' you fret none."

"I know. You must think I have no faith at all, the number of times I've asked you about those papers."

Barnabas grinned. "No suh. You a man o' faith, all right. Otherwise, why you be lookin' over 'cross the meadow a hundred times a day? Mm hm, I seen you—yo' eyes hungry, searchin', expectin', waitin'. It take faith to believe she comin' back."

Colton pursed his lips. The man was downright uncanny sometimes in the way he could look straight through Colton and see his whole being laid out like a page in a book. Barnabas might not be able to read words, but there weren't too many men Colton knew who could read hearts.

He rubbed his hand over his chin. "She's back."

Barnabas threw his head back in a deep, rich, joyous laugh. "See there? Who says you ain't got no faith?"

Chapter 15

Colton walked out of the post office and tucked a letter from his parents into his vest pocket, saving it to share with Barnabas over a cup of coffee. He crossed the street to the general store.

"Mornin', Clyde."

"Howdy, Colton. I'll be right with you. Sweet Pea has me rearranging these shelves."

Betsy cackled. "If I can get Clyde to move faster than a snail."

"No hurry. I'll just help myself to the peppermint sticks." Colton grinned and stuck his hand in the glass jar on the counter.

Clyde dusted his hands on his apron. "What brings you to town today, Colton?"

"I had a letter to mail to my mother and father back in Tucker's Gap." He patted the envelope in his pocket. "Mother must have had the same idea."

He didn't mention his other errand—stopping by the land office. He loved Clyde and Betsy dearly, but Betsy didn't always know when to keep information to herself.

Clyde nodded. "What can we get for you today, my friend?"

Colton sucked on the peppermint stick. "Pound of coffee, couple bars of lye soap, tin of sorghum, and a can of neat's-foot oil."

Clyde gathered the items and ciphered the total. "Anything else?"

He pulled the sweet confection from his mouth and pointed it at Clyde. "Half dozen peppermints sticks. And a box of cartridges—twenty-two caliber, rim fire."

Clyde set the box of ammunition on the counter beside the other items. "Fixin' to do some huntin'?" He caught Colton's eye. "Or are you expectin' trouble?"

Colton bit off the end of the peppermint stick. "Just bein' prepared."

Betsy came around the end of the counter, glancing this way and that. Nobody else was in the store. "You know that fancy-pants lawyer that was nosing around?"

Colton counted out the money for his purchases. "Maxwell Rayburn. What about him?"

"He's back." Betsy pressed her lips into a tight line and gave a single nod. "He was in here this morning. Wanted to order some expensive cigars. I don't trust him. His eyes are too close together."

Clyde guffawed. "Sweet Pea doesn't like him because he called our store a second-rate establishment." Clyde leaned forward, propping his elbows on the counter. "I'd like to know why he was orderin' them ceegars here. Does that mean he plans to stick around instead of goin' back to Athens?"

Colton gathered his purchases and pondered Clyde's

question. "I'd like to know the answer to that one myself. See y'all Sunday."

He walked across the street where he had left Jasper and tucked his purchases into his saddlebags. With a pat on the horse's neck, Colton mounted and reined the gelding around to the other side of town. The land office sat tucked behind the newspaper office where Colton could tether Jasper without Betsy peeking out the front window of the general store and letting her imagination run rampant.

The front door stood open to catch whatever breeze might be stirring. Colton stepped inside. A slight man with garters around his sleeves sat at the desk, his balding head bent over his work and his spectacles perched lopsided on his nose.

"Mornin'," Colton greeted the man.

The little man's glasses slid to one side when he jerked his head up. He caught them before they hit the desk. "Good morning, good morning." He set his pen aside and rose. "Mr....Danville? No, no, don't tell me." He studied Colton through squinty eyes. "Danford? No, Daniels? No..." He tapped his finger on his nose. "Ah! Dalton! I knew I'd think of it. I never forget a name or a face."

"Uh, yes." Colton held in the chuckle that tried to snuffle out. "You're Mr. Kimber, right?"

"Randall Kimber, at your service." He straightened his shoulders. "And what can I do for you today, Mr. Danville?"

Colton's lips twisted into a half smile. "I was hoping you could give me some information." He gestured toward the map on the wall. "May I?"

"Of course, of course." Mr. Kimber stepped aside while Colton moved over to the map and pointed to a section.

"My land is right here." He tapped his finger on the forty-acre section a half mile from the Chestatee River, then slid his finger over to trace the massive area behind his land. "I understand this section of timber is for sale."

Mr. Kimber shook his head. "No, no, not for sale anymore. That thousand-acre tract has been purchased. Sorry if you were interested in buying it yourself, Mr. Darnell. You're a little late."

Colton tried to appear disappointed. "Oh? Someone's already bought it?"

"That's right, that's right." Kimber bobbed his head. "None other than, uh—Theodore Bolden." He appeared pleased with himself for having such an important tidbit of information. "Prime timberland, prime—from what I'm told. I've never actually seen the land myself."

"I see." Despite Mr. Kimber's mistake on the first name, there was no mistaking Thaddeus Bolden was the "old family friend" of whom Auralie's brother spoke. Uneasiness poked Colton's gut. If Bolden's men went in there and began clear-cutting, they'd destroy the watershed. "Did Mr. Bolden happen to say when he plans to start cutting timber?"

"Oh, no, no." Kimber's head wobbled from side to side. "Mr. Bolden wasn't here himself. It was his lawyer—a Mr....uh, Radford, and of course, Mr. Tom Covingdale, Mr. Bolden's representative."

"Dale Covington?"

"Yes, yes, that's what I said."

Colton swallowed the remark he wanted to make, and it had nothing to do with Mr. Kimber's inability to remember names. "Did Mr. Covington or Mr. Rayburn make any mention of building a sawmill on the property?"

Mr. Kimber scratched his head. "No, no. Not that I recall." A smug smile slid across his features. "And I have an excellent memory if I do say so myself."

"Thank you, Mr. Kimber. Good day."

"Good day to you, Mr. Davenport."

Colton exited the office, pausing by the hitching rail to ponder the revelation. If Bolden had no plans to operate an on-site sawmill, how did he intend on transporting the timber? Dale Covington's skillful sidestepping of Colton's earlier question stirred an uncomfortable inkling in his stomach. He gritted his teeth with the realization he was about to clash with the Covington and Bolden clans.

"Hey Colton. Hold up a minute."

Colton pulled his thoughts out of the shadowy recesses of speculation and looked up. Jack McCaffey headed in his direction, striding with purpose.

"Hey Jack."

Jack held out his hand with its ever-present ink stains. They shook hands and Jack lowered his voice. "There's something I've learned that I think you need to know. Normally, I wouldn't divulge this kind of information until it comes out in the *Sentinel,* but I believe it's going to impact you personally. Thought you might want to know before you read about it in the paper."

The wariness that pricked Colton in the land office heightened. "I'm listening."

Jack glanced over his shoulder toward the land office. "Did Kimber tell you about the land deal out by your place?"

"If you mean Bolden buying up the timberland that borders my property, yes. Is there something else?"

"I have a few sources from all over the state, and I've recently been in touch with a couple of them who have contacts within the Georgia Railroad and Banking Company."

Colton shrugged. "Spur only comes as far north as Athens. What's that got to do with us?"

Jack quirked an eyebrow. "You know the Boldens and Covingtons are thick as thieves and twice as crafty. According to my sources, Covington has a contact or two at the Georgia Railroad who owe him a political favor in exchange for some dealings that went on under the table a while back." Jack flapped his hand, apparently dismissing the history to get to the meat of the issue. "Seems Covington is pulling some strings to bring the spur from Athens up into our neck of the woods—literally."

"I remember reading about his campaign promises in the *Sentinel* a couple of weeks ago, but you know how politicians are. They'll spout just about anything to get elected." Colton propped one elbow on his hand and stroked his chin. "Is this spur extension he's talking about related to that tract of timber Bolden just purchased?"

"Bolden needs a way to ship timber to the mills south of here."

Colton rolled the information over and met Jack's pointed look. "You know why Covington and his team of surveyors were taking calculations across my land, don't you?"

Jack turned his palms up and lifted his shoulders. "All I can say is, if it were me, I'd make a trip to the county seat and make sure my land deed was properly recorded."

Auralie ran her finger across the leather spines of the dozens of books occupying the shelves in Belle's parlor. Every title she touched brought back the memory of Dale's face when he scooped the McGuffey's off the ground and glowered at her, knowing her intent. Surely one of these volumes was appropriate for teaching Barnabas to read.

"Have you become bored with *Wuthering Heights*?"

Auralie glanced up and found Belle eyeing her from across the room. Her copy of *Wuthering Heights*—with a ribbon marking her place halfway through the book—lay on the chair she'd occupied earlier.

"No. I just thought I'd look and see what else you have."

Belle rose and crossed to the bookcase. "What are you looking for?"

"Something…simple."

Belle cocked her head. "Simple? That's odd since you were always the one with her nose stuck in a book when we were in our adolescence."

Auralie shrugged off Belle's observation and fluttered her fingers. "I wondered if you might have something light and easy to read."

Her cousin narrowed her eyes. "Auralie, what are you up to?"

"Who says I'm up to anything?" She didn't want to engage in a debate of the moral rights or wrongs of teaching a black man to read.

"Perhaps because I know you better than anyone." She plunked her hands on her hips. "And perhaps because I remember the trouble you got into when you were a kid teaching the slaves to read." She glanced out the front window that looked out across the meadow. "You aren't thinking what I think you're thinking, are you?"

"Belle, I—"

"Stop and consider what you're doing, Auralie. Most people frown on teaching Negros to read, whether they're free or not." The pleading tone in Belle's voice pinched Auralie's heart.

A heavy sigh escaped and she crossed to take up her copy of *Wuthering Heights* again. Controlling her frustration, she settled into the chair. "I'm quite aware of the public opinion. I happen to disagree."

Belle thrust her hands out to her sides. "There are thousands of white people who can't read."

Auralie nodded. "Yes, but in most cases, they don't care to learn. They weren't denied the privilege."

"You taught Mammy to read, didn't you?"

Auralie sucked in a breath. For years, she and Mammy kept their secret, and it thrilled her every time she saw Mammy pick up the Bible. "Yes. It's a blessing to know she can read God's Word for herself. I don't regret it."

"Does your father know she can read?"

"Of course not." She stood and approached the window where Belle still stood. "You know what would happen if he found out."

"Auralie, you're asking for trouble." Belle returned her gaze to the bookcase. "I don't think I have anything here you can use."

Auralie's heart grieved the silence between her and Belle in the carriage all the way to church. The space in the carriage echoed, devoid of their usual chatter and teasing. Even at the dinner table last night their stilted conversation remained limited to the weather and other inane topics. They'd been so close all their lives. How could one disagreement carve such a chasm between them?

Sam halted the carriage in front of the church and hastened to help the ladies disembark. Auralie followed Belle into the church and found their seats just as the service was beginning. She glanced across the aisle where Colton generally sat.

The black wool coat Colton normally wore to church was absent, no doubt due to the warmer temperatures. Instead, he sat in his shirtsleeves and string tie, looking as handsome as ever, except for the scowl on his face. He appeared as troubled as Auralie felt. She longed to press her fingers to his brow and smooth out the worries she saw etched there, but she didn't know what to do with her own burdens. How could she expect to comfort Colton, for whom she cared so much?

He glanced over at her, as if he could feel her gaze upon

him. A small smile tipped the corners of his mouth. The now-familiar tingle she felt every time Colton smiled tip-toed through her.

She shifted her gaze to Belle who sat stiffly beside her. She didn't wish to cause her cousin distress. Perhaps it was time for her to go home. The only trouble was Covington Plantation didn't feel like home, and she couldn't look out the window there and see Colton's sheep and cornfield.

After the hymn singing, Pastor Shuford stepped into the pulpit and invited the congregation to open their Bibles to the book of Matthew, chapter twenty-five. Auralie followed along as he read the words of Jesus, describing the ministering to the hungry, thirsty, naked, and lonely.

"'And the King shall answer and say unto them, Verily I say unto you, Inasmuch as ye have done it unto one of the least of these my brethren, ye have done it unto me.'"

Pastor Shuford went on to explain giving from the heart and expecting nothing in return, seeking injustices and remedying them with no thought to self. The preacher challenged his flock to find someone to whom they could minister—someone who could not reciprocate.

Auralie soaked up the words like a dry sponge. How she'd fretted her lack of purpose, the absence of usefulness, her china doll existence. Her heart cried out to God. *Lord, use me. Let my hands be filled with something worthwhile to minister to those who have no means to repay a kindness—unto the least of these.* Moisture burned her eyes and she blinked, but a tear escaped anyway. She discreetly dashed it away. She closed her eyes during the final prayer and inquired at God's throne if teaching people like Mammy and Barnabas to read was her calling.

When she opened her eyes, she found Belle looking at her with a mixture of confusion and pain in her expression. The congregation began filing out, pausing at the door to shake the preacher's hand. The line moved slowly and just before she arrived at the door, she felt fingers squeeze hers. She glanced down. Belle held fast to her hand.

They greeted Pastor Shuford and thanked him, then made their way to the carriage.

"Allow me."

The voice Auralie heard in her dreams turned her head. Colton stepped over and offered his hand. She placed her hand in his, and his smile sent butterfly wings fluttering through her middle.

He swept his hat off. "It's nice to see you, Auralie."

Her breath caught, and for a moment she forgot where she was. If only she could feel the touch of his hand and hear him utter her name every day for the rest of her life. For the briefest of moments, she wondered if God would mind if she'd add that to her prayer.

"It's nice seeing you as well...Colton."

Belle cleared her throat, rattling Auralie's consciousness. Colton still held her hand. A rush of heat skittered up her neck into her face.

Colton handed her up into the carriage and aided Belle up as well. He fidgeted with the brim of his hat. "I'd like to talk to you sometime. If that's all right."

Auralie gave him a soft smile. "I'd like that. Perhaps tomorrow?"

Colton nodded. "I could come by."

Auralie's smile widened, and the heat in her face intensified. "I think I'd like to meet you at the pasture. I love watching the lambs."

"That'd be fine." Colton took a step backward. "Until tomorrow." And the carriage pulled away.

She and Belle rode in silence for a couple of minutes before her cousin spoke. "I saw your tears in church." She reached across the seat and covered Auralie's hand with hers. "I really didn't understand."

"I know." Auralie swallowed hard. "I'm not sure I understood myself. Do you remember when I complained to you about not having a purpose except to be nothing more than a china doll?"

Belle smiled. "I remember."

"And do you remember when you said you wanted me to see how it could be if I did my own choosing?"

Belle's smile deepened. "I remember that, too."

Auralie twisted around in her seat to face Belle. "Well, I've decided to let God do my choosing for me."

Chapter 16

Auralie clutched the storybook close to her heart. "Oh Belle, how can I ever thank you?"

Belle dabbed a tear away from her eye and shrugged. "No thank-you is necessary. As I told you after church yesterday—I understand now." She touched the book with her fingertips. "This was mine when I was little. I was saving it for when I had children, but—" She slipped both arms around Auralie. "There's no reason why you can't use it now."

A thrill ran through Auralie. Her cousin understood—really understood. "Belle, I'll never forget this." She gave her a squeeze. "I can't wait to show Colton."

"Well then, go." Belle laughed and pushed her away. She flapped her hands, shooing Auralie out the door.

Invisible wings carried Auralie across the meadow. In the distance, Colton worked on the rail fence that divided the sheep pasture from the cornfield. This time, her brother wouldn't stop her. Excitement bubbled within her at the prospect of opening Barnabas's eyes to the world of written words.

"Colton!" She waved when he looked up.

He returned her wave and came to meet her. "You're certainly in a joyful disposition this morning."

Breathless from hurrying, she beamed at him. "Yes, I am." She held out the storybook. "I hope Barnabas won't be offended, but the words in this book are easy, and until he learns how the letters sound and—"

Colton held up his hand. "Whoa." He laughed. "There's no need for apology. This is a very kind thing you're doing." He glanced toward the Hancock home. "Are you sure it's all right with your cousin? Some folks don't approve."

Auralie tilted her head and gave him a nod. "At first, she didn't understand my desire to see people like Barnabas learn to read. But after yesterday's sermon, she had a change of heart."

"Ah, 'unto the least of these'." Colton smiled.

Her throat tightened. "This book belonged to Belle when she was little. She was saving it for her own children."

"Then we shall take very good care of it so we can return it to her in good condition." He reached out and grasped her hand. "Come on. Barnabas is repairing the lean-to."

The warmth and gentle strength of his hand quickened her pulse and set butterflies loose in her middle.

As they neared the cabin, Colton grinned down at her then hollered for Barnabas. A moment later, the former slave stuck his head out of the lean-to.

"Wha'sa matter, Mistah Colton?" He set his tools down and trotted around the corner of the house. He stopped short when he saw Auralie. "Miz Covington." He dipped his head.

Bursting with excitement, Auralie motioned to the bench and rockers on the front porch. "Let's sit down."

Barnabas shifted his feet, obviously uncomfortable being seated in Auralie's presence. She looked up at him and gestured toward the bench. "Please."

He eyed the book in her hands, and she turned it so he could see the front. "Barnabas, I realize this is a child's book and you're a man. But this book is a wonderful starting place for learning to read. If you'd like, I'd love to teach you." Her heart leaped for joy when his eyes widened and a slow, broad smile stretched across his face.

"You hear dat, Mistah Colton?" His deep voice broke. "I's gonna learn to read!"

Auralie's heart swelled with joy until she wasn't sure her body could contain it. She swiped at a tear and opened the book to the first page.

Colton hated leaving the next morning, especially after watching Barnabas's face glow when he read his first word—*dog*. But he decided to take Jack McCaffey's advice and confirm the land deed records at the county seat. He rode into Mount Yonah by midafternoon. The building being used temporarily to house the county records wasn't hard to find. A crude sign nailed above the door declared it the courthouse, even though it in no way resembled such a building. The residents of the county seat proudly anticipated the completion of the official new courthouse—a fine brick building—before the year was out. In the meantime, the ramshackle framed structure before him served as county offices and courtroom, if it didn't fall down first.

Colton stabled Jasper and then strode back to the courthouse. Two dirty windows at either end of the building allowed in muted light. A man sat at a desk in the corner with his back to the door, diligently laboring over paperwork.

Colton removed his hat. "Excuse me."

The man looked over his shoulder and turned the paper he was working on facedown. "Yessir, can I help you?"

"Yes, you may. I need to look up the recording of a forty-acre tract of land down near Juniper Springs."

The clerk rose from his chair, his legs bumping it backwards. His blond hair splayed out in multiple directions. "J-Juniper Springs, you say?"

Colton laid his hat on a long table that sat under one of the grimy windows. "That's right. It would have been recorded in March of 1856. Where might I find that record book?"

The clerk fumbled through two shelves of bound journals, pulling one out and pushing it back in, stacking three on the desk and then replacing them. Colton watched him, nonplussed. He assumed the records were all kept in chronological order. Finally, after shuffling several volumes, the young man pulled out the book that lay on the bottom of the stack—the one that had sat on the corner of the desk when Colton entered.

"Here it is. What would you like me to look up for you?"

The clerk's nervous mannerisms and disorganization raised Colton's suspicion. "If you don't mind, I'd rather look up the entry myself. These records are all public, are they not?"

"Well, yes…but, uh, some of the records aren't completed yet, so you might not be able to find them."

"Not completed?" Colton's eyebrows rose along with his misgivings. "The record I'm looking for dates back over four years ago. Seems to me there's been ample time to record the deed."

He stepped forward and reached for the volume in the clerk's hands, but the young man held on to it. Beads of sweat popped out on the fellow's forehead and upper lip. Colton kept his voice even but firm.

"Sir, as a citizen of this county, I have the right to search any of these public records. I really don't want to go get the constable, but I will if I have to."

The clerk reluctantly released the book and pressed his lips into a tight, thin line. Colton carried the journal to the table under the window. He turned pages until he found February 1856. He ran his finger down to the end of the page. The next page bore two listings entered at the end of March, and then the rest of the page contained April records.

Odd. Colton remembered the day like it was yesterday. Pastor Winslow had told Colton he knew his time on this earth was growing short, and he wanted all his affairs in order. Colton still recalled the grief that sliced through him at his dear friend's announcement. The two of them had come to the county seat together, and Colton had watched as the preacher recorded his will, and signed over ownership of his land to Colton.

He turned to get the clerk's attention, only to find him standing a few steps away, watching over Colton's shoulder. "There seems to be a page missing. March 12, 1856."

The young man wiped his hands on his pants. "Uh, that's...that was before I worked here." An unmistakable tremor resonated in his voice.

Colton stood and crossed his arms over his chest. "Are you not responsible for all the records in this office, those established before you were employed as well as after?"

Muscles in the clerk's neck twitched and he blanched.

Pieces of the puzzle didn't all quite fit together yet, but Colton was getting a clearer picture of how they were cut. "I don't know what's going on here, but I do know this." He stabbed his finger on the open pages of the book he'd been examining. "All that juggling around of the books you did was meant to cover up the fact that this ledger was already on your desk when I walked in." He slid his finger along the bound edge of the pages where they joined the spine. "It's not hard to see a page has been torn out. Is that what you were working on when I came in? Is that the paper you turned over so I wouldn't see it?"

The clerk's eyes shifted to and fro. When he thrust his hand out, it trembled. "I don't know what you're talking about. I just work here and do as I'm told."

"And who told you to tear out that page? Was it Maxwell Rayburn?"

A droplet of sweat dribbled down the clerk's temple. He appeared about to crumple in a heap on the floor. "I don't know anyone by that name."

Colton stuck his thumbs in his pockets. "Are you going to let me see that page you were working on?"

"No. Th–that's—it's, uh, confidential."

Anger churned in Colton's stomach, but no good would come of him losing his temper. "I don't know how much you were paid to alter these records, but it's not worth going to jail." He closed the ledger and tucked it under his arm, picked up his hat, and started for the door.

"Wait! Where are you taking that book?"

Colton turned. The fellow looked like he was going to be sick.

"To the constable's office. Would you like come along?"

"Look, mister, I was just following orders."

Colton shifted the volume to the other arm. "Whose orders?"

All the fight seeped out of the young clerk, who probably only saw the altering of the records as a chance to make some extra money. He blew out a stiff breath. "By order of Shelby Covington."

* * *

Auralie and Belle carried their teacups to the side porch and settled into the comfortable chairs. The latest edition of the *Sentinel* lay on the small table between them. The headline proclaimed Shelby Covington's political ambitions and promises. The words sent conflicting emotions swirling in Auralie's stomach.

"I've come to realize this arranged marriage to Perry is but one piece in a monumental quagmire. Father is using me as a pawn in a political game of chess." She set her teacup on the table. "He wants the governor's mansion, and he'll use whatever means necessary to get there."

Belle settled her cup into its saucer. "I hate to think Uncle Shelby would do such a thing, but I'm afraid you're right. What are you going to do?"

Auralie released a sigh. "I don't know. After months of fretting and weeks of praying, I think I've finally placed the issue in God's hands. Now if I can just leave it there—"

She avoided filling in the blank. The truth was she still struggled with doubts, but if her faith were ever to grow, fully trusting God with every part of her life was the answer.

A muffled sniff sounded from Belle. Auralie turned and found her cousin blotting away a tear with her napkin. Between being in the family way and missing her husband, her cousin's weepiness attacked with regularity. Auralie reached over to pat Belle's hand.

"Missing Lloyd?"

Belle sniffed again. "Yes, but I'm frightened, too." She gestured to the newspaper. "Did you read the article on page two? The one about the state militia?"

Auralie shook her head. "I know there's been talk."

"They're saying they aren't waiting to see who will win the election, and they're beginning to form a state militia now." Belle swallowed, her effort to be brave evident. "They say they want to be ready in case Lincoln is elected and Georgia secedes. Lloyd mentioned in his last letter that a lot of men are signing up already."

"Did he say he plans to sign up?"

"No, but I fear that's what he's implying."

Auralie squeezed Belle's hand. "But he doesn't know about the baby yet. That will make a difference, won't it?"

Belle laid her hand over her abdomen, a gesture Auralie had often seen her do. "I hope so."

As so often happened, Auralie's gaze drifted toward Colton's place. Sheep dotted the pasture like scattered clumps of snow. She wondered silently if he would enlist in the militia if conflict arose. What a difficult decision. Would he fight to defend Georgia? Every time she heard the topic debated, the outcry was always for state's rights, but in truth, one of the rights for which they clamored was the right to own slaves. She couldn't imagine Colton fighting *for* slavery.

Belle flicked a mosquito from her arm. "Do you think the forming of the militia will affect your father's election?"

Auralie lifted her shoulders. "I don't know. Dale has announced he intends to stand up for Georgia and defend her rights. Father was incensed. He kept telling Dale he could send 'a couple of darkies' in his place, but Dale rejected that. He said he would purchase a commission and be an officer."

Belle's mouth dropped open. "But he and Gwendolyn are going to be married next month. Surely he wouldn't go off to join the militia and leave his bride."

"That's what he said." Auralie sipped her now cooled tea. "I don't know what Gwendolyn thinks about it."

The sound of hoofbeats coming up the drive drew their attention, and Auralie's heart turned over in anticipation.

Perhaps Colton had returned from the trip he'd told her he was making to the county seat. She stood and smoothed her skirt. Glancing at her reflection in the window, she gave her hair a pat and pinched her cheeks.

Belle winked at her and led the way around the corner of the porch. But it wasn't Colton. Reuben, one of her father's slaves dismounted from a tired, old gray plow horse. The blood in Auralie's veins ran cold, and she stood rooted in place. Reuben tied the horse and approached the porch. He lowered his eyes and gave a polite nod.

"Miss Covington. I has a note fo' you from yo' mothah." He held out an ivory envelope with her mother's distinctive handwriting.

Auralie stared at the folded missive as if it were a snake. Her feet wouldn't move. Her fingers of her left hand found the ring on her right and twisted it in vicious circles.

Belle stepped forward and took the note. "Thank you. If you'd like to go around to the summer kitchen, I'm sure Maizie will give you some refreshment and Sam will water your horse."

Reuben bobbed his head. "Thank ya kindly, ma'am." He disappeared around the corner of the house.

Belle turned with the letter in her hand. "You have to read it."

Auralie shook her head, as if the vehemence of the motion would keep the words of the letter at bay. But as much as she wanted to pretend it didn't exist, she couldn't tear her eyes from the envelope.

"It's happening." Her own voice sounded like it belonged to someone else. Her prayers had found their way to God's throne room, she was sure of it. He heard the cry of her heart. She'd said that very morning she intended to trust Him with every part of her life. The moment of truth had arrived, and she had a choice. She could cling to God in faith, or she could crumble.

Mammy came bustling through the side door. "Reuben jus' came to the back do', and he say he brung a—"

Mammy's groan sounded like glass breaking.

Auralie took the note and slid her finger under the edge to break the seal. With Mammy on one side of her and Belle on the other, she read her mother's words.

Auralie,
Perry Bolden has telegraphed from New York. His ship has docked, and he plans to take the southbound train scheduled to leave for Charleston on Thursday, May 31st.

May thirty-first. Perry was boarding the train today to come home. Auralie's stomach churned, but she continued to read.

After attending to some business in Charleston, he will take the train to Augusta where a carriage will meet him and bring him home. He plans to arrive by June the 5th. A carriage will be sent for you on Monday, June 4th.
Mother

Auralie crumpled the note in her hand. As much as it pained her, she owed it to Colton to be honest with him.

Chapter 17

"Engaged?"

Colton almost choked on the word. His delight at seeing Auralie coming through the meadow with the morning sun playing off her hair evaporated. The impact of her statement left him reeling.

"Colton, I'm so sorry I didn't tell you sooner." She leaned against one of the apple trees and twisted her ring. "At first, I didn't think it was appropriate to even mention it. You and I were barely acquainted."

He stared at her, but she wouldn't look him in the eye. Instead, her gaze shifted everywhere except at him.

"After a while, I kept telling myself the engagement wasn't official until it was announced." She tipped her head. "After we became…friends, I didn't want to read more into the friendship than was truly there."

Colton hadn't yet attempted to put into words what was truly there, but he knew without a doubt that it went beyond friendship. Pain sliced through his heart and realization overtook him. *I'm in love with her.*

"Every time I intended to tell you, I simply…couldn't." Her voice reflected her troubled spirit.

If he reacted in anger, he would only confirm to her what he now knew. He found his tongue. "I hope you didn't think I'd not want you to be with the man you love."

"But I don't." Strained emotion clouded her tone and her eyes misted.

Confusion caught Colton off balance. "I don't understand. You don't want to be with your fiancé?"

She caught her lip in her teeth. Anguish—the kind born of long, silent suffering—veiled her eyes. Her voice fell to a whisper carried away by the wind. "I don't love him."

Her conflicting statements defied understanding. Colton ran his hand through his hair. "Am I to understand you're marrying a man you don't love?" He had no business asking her such a question, but he couldn't help himself.

The flush in her cheeks evidenced the humiliation racing through her at having made such a declaration. A war raged within him. Part of him longed to take her in his arms and comfort her, tell her she need not say any more. But another part of him he hadn't known existed until now wanted to confront her and demand to know why she waited until he'd fallen in love with her before telling him she was promised to another.

The lines in her brow furrowed and her voice bore a brittle tone. "Do you remember the day we met?"

How could he forget? He'd literally tripped over her. He nodded and she went on.

"I heard some men in the café that day call out to you, but there was so much commotion. I thought they'd called you Bolden."

Colton rolled back his memory to that day. He recalled the misunderstanding.

"I haven't seen my fiancé since we were children. I can't even remember what he looks like. My father and his father arranged this union four years ago. He's been studying abroad for the past five years, and now…" The tremble in her voice punctuated her unfinished sentence.

Now? Understanding dawned as all the pieces of the puzzle fit together into an unspeakable portrait of Shelby Covington's selfishness and greed. The man was a canker on everything that being a man, a husband, and a father meant.

"Your father has arranged for you to marry Thaddeus Bolden's son?"

Twin tears slipped from Auralie's eyes, and she nodded. "I've received a letter from my mother telling me that Perry is arriving tomorrow and I must return home." She grimaced as if she'd just tasted something bitter. "A carriage is being sent for me later this morning. I've come to tell you good-bye."

Acid gall rose in his throat as an invisible fist punched him in the gut. His hand reached out involuntarily for her, to pull her to him, but she took a step back. She clasped her hands together under her chin, her arms clamped tightly to her chest.

"Auralie, I—"

"Don't." She shook her head, as if afraid to hear what was in his heart. "Please encourage Barnabas to keep learning. And take care of those lambs." She covered her mouth with trembling fingers that muffled her words. "I'll miss you."

She picked up her skirts and ran through the orchard and across the field toward the Hancock home.

"Mistah Colton?"

Colton turned. Barnabas stood a few yards away, his expression one of sorrow as he watched Auralie leaving. "I's sorry, Mistah Colton, but I needs to tell yo' some o' the sheeps is missin'. Free was barkin', and when I went to see about it, there be a place in the fence where that orn'ry ram musta busted through. Free wouldn't leave the rest of the sheeps."

Colton gazed another long moment in Auralie's direction, wondering if his heart would ever be whole again, before he turned to join Barnabas.

The lump in Auralie's throat nearly prevented her from drawing a breath as the carriage pulled away from Belle's. The sobs she'd valiantly tried to hold back won the battle as tears cascaded down her cheeks.

Mammy slipped her arm around Auralie and drew her close. "There, there, baby, don' you cry. You have me cryin', too." She rocked Auralie back and forth in a comforting motion. "Shhhh."

"Mammy, I did what you said. I prayed and asked God to intervene, to provide a way out of this marriage. Every day and night I begged God for help, but He didn't answer."

"Why you think He don't answer? Jus' 'cause He don't answer the way you want Him to, don't mean He ain't list'nin'." Mammy pulled a handkerchief from her sleeve and blotted Auralie's tears. "Maybe His answer is to change you 'stead o' changin' what happenin' around you. Ever' time a prayer leave yo' lips, yo' faith and trust grow. You know God hear you, He care, and He never leave you."

Auralie clung to Mammy. The woman's wisdom fell over Auralie like a gentle rain washing away her doubts. Until now, she'd not tried to define God's promises to her. In that heartbeat, she knew…He loved her. Did that mean He'd answer her prayer the way she hoped? She didn't know that yet. She did know a deeper level of trust she never before knew existed now reinforced her, regardless of what lay ahead.

Mammy squeezed her shoulders. "We jus' keep on prayin', honey girl. Sweet Lawd Jesus, please hear us. We need a touch from Yo' hand, a miracle."

A miracle. Would God grant her a miracle if she asked?

"Whoa, there!" Their driver, Reuben, called out to the horses and the carriage lurched to a stop.

Auralie and Mammy exchanged alarmed looks. "What is it, Reuben? What's the problem?"

"Trouble ahead, miss."

Auralie stuck her head out the side of the carriage and craned her neck to see what was going on. On the road just ahead, a man jerked a black man from the wooded area along the road and dragged him toward a tethered horse. Auralie's heart seized. *Barnabas!*

"Reuben, drive on up there so I can speak to that man."

"Could be dangerous, miss."

Auralie pointed. "Go."

"Yes'm." Reuben clucked to the horses.

Mammy leaned to the side. "What goin' on? Who that man be?"

Auralie glanced back at her. "I'm not sure who he is, but he has Barnabas."

The carriage pulled alongside the two men and halted. Auralie called to the man. "You there. What do you think you're doing?"

Barnabas looked up at her with an expression that made the hair stand up on the back of her neck.

The burly man with greasy hair and an unkempt beard pulled a pair of shackles from his saddlebags and clamped them on Barnabas's wrists. "Pickin' up strays, ma'am. Ain't no concern o' your'n."

Indignation straightened her spine. "It most certainly is my concern if I witness you taking a free man captive."

The white man guffawed and called Barnabas a vulgar name. "Why else would a darkie be hidin' in the woods if he ain't runnin'?"

"I weren't runnin', Miz Cov—"

The man backhanded Barnabas. He staggered backward and blood trickled from the corner of his mouth.

"Shut up." The white man yanked a bowie knife from his belt. "Open your mouth again and I'll slit your tongue."

"Stop that. Don't you dare hit him again." Wrath flamed through Auralie, and she climbed from the carriage. "See here. I happen to know this man is not a runaway."

The bounty hunter smirked. "I say he is. The man I work for will pay me a nice bounty for every darkie I bring in." He swept his hat off and held it over his heart, bowing in a sarcastic demonstration of mock respect. "Beggin' pardon, ma'am."

Auralie gritted her teeth. "Who is the man who pays you to capture men like this?"

He plopped his hat back on his head. "My boss, the honorable Shelby Covington. He hired me to recover his property. Escaped slaves make me a tidy profit."

Bile rose in Auralie's throat and her stomach twisted. "I'm telling you this man is not an escaped slave. He works for—"

"I ain't interested in no petticoat pardon." He cinched a rope around the wrist shackles on Barnabas's arms and slid the other end through an iron ring attached to his saddle.

Mammy stood in the carriage and shook her finger at the man. "You watch yo' mouth. This here is a lady, and—"

The man pulled the knife again and brandished it toward Mammy. "Lady, huh? Well, lady, you need to teach your darkie some manners. Or I can do it for you."

Auralie tried to swallow, but fear choked her. She watched in horror as the man mounted his horse and jerked on the rope to pull Barnabas along.

"Where are you taking him?"

The man's sneer revealed tobacco-stained teeth. "Back where the overseer'll teach him not to run no more." He nudged his horse into a trot, forcing Barnabas to run behind the animal.

Auralie whirled toward the carriage. Both Mammy and Reuben wore pained grimaces. "Reuben, turn around and take the north road."

"But missy, massah say to bring you home."

"I'll tell him you were obeying my instructions." She picked up her skirts and clambered into the conveyance. "The north road, Reuben. Hurry!"

Reuben turned the carriage around and sent the horses running full tilt, veering to the left at the fork, onto the north road. The wind pulled at Auralie's hair, but she wouldn't let Reuben slow the horses until Colton's place came into view.

"Stop!"

Reuben pulled back on the reins to bring the heaving horses to a halt. Auralie discarded propriety and jumped down.

"Colton! Colton!" She picked up her skirts and ran toward the house, screaming Colton's name, but he didn't appear. She ran down the slope toward the cornfield.

"Colton!"

"Auralie?"

She halted and searched in the direction of his voice. He came jogging toward her from the sheep pasture. She ran to meet him.

Trepidation edged his voice. "What's wrong?"

"Barnabas. A bounty hunter took him." She gasped for breath. "Come quickly."

He grasped her hand. "Some of the sheep got out. We split up to look for them." Together they hurried back toward the house. He sent a sweeping search in the direction Auralie's carriage had come. "Where?"

Nausea swirled in her stomach. "Covington Plantation."

Colton's jaw dropped, his expression incredulous. "You go ahead. As soon as I throw a saddle on Jasper I'll catch up with you." He turned and ran back toward the barn.

"Hurry, Colton!"

He called back to her over his shoulder. "I will. Go on. Jasper will catch up with the carriage before you get there."

She dashed back to the carriage where Reuben waited to help her aboard. As soon as she was seated, Reuben turned the team around and lit out back down the road. The distance to Covington Plantation normally took an hour at a more sedate pace, but Reuben encouraged the horses to keep moving.

"Oh dear Lord, don't let us be too late. Please don't let them hurt Barnabas."

Mammy gripped Auralie's hand. "Amen."

When they were within a mile of the entrance, the sound of pounding hoofbeats coming up behind them turned Auralie's head. Colton's sweat-flecked chestnut gelding pulled abreast of the carriage, and he adjusted the horse's speed to keep pace.

Reuben steered the horses through the huge iron gate that yawned open. Colton went ahead and skidded his horse to a stop. He vaulted from the saddle and ran to meet the carriage as the lathered horses halted by the front entrance. He seized Auralie around the waist and swung her to the ground. Grabbing her hand, they ran up the front steps to the wide veranda.

Her father stepped through the open French doors from the parlor with a brandy snifter in his hand. "Auralie," he barked. "What is the meaning of this?"

For once, Father's intimidating growl had no effect on her. "Father, a bounty hunter who says he was hired by you has taken this man's friend. Barnabas isn't a runaway. He doesn't even belong to you. Colton bought him and freed him."

Father turned his glower on Colton. "I know who you are. You're Danfield."

"That's right, and what your daughter says is true. Barnabas is no longer your property and carries papers to prove it, but it seems your bounty hunter took him anyway. I demand to know where he is."

"You demand? Who do you think you're talking to? And take your hand off my daughter."

Instead of complying, Colton tightened his grip on Auralie's hand.

Another man, with thick auburn hair and a daunting, chiseled countenance, stepped out the door behind Father. He scowled from Auralie to Colton and back again.

In the next heartbeat, everyone began talking at once.

"Auralie, how dare you, coming racing in here like a hooligan—"

"Father, please—"

"Covington, I demand you release Barnabas immediately."

"Who is this man, and why does he have hold of my fiancée's hand?"

Auralie drew a sharp breath. Fiancée? Didn't Mother's note say he was to arrive tomorrow? The tall man with the brooding eyes and sinister brows leveled a glare at her. Perry Bolden raked a disapproving scowl over her.

"I don't understand this at all. This can't be Auralie."

He turned to look at her father. "You assured me that my future wife was delicate and refined and conducted herself with elegance and decorum." He tossed a disdainful look at Auralie. "I'm appalled at this unladylike behavior."

"How dare you insinuate that I misled you? I am highly offended. Why, she—"

"Covington, answer me. I want to know where Barnabas is right now."

Perry frowned at her again. "Where is the pink silk gown you were instructed to wear upon my arrival? And who is this—this famer with whom you are consorting?" He shook his head and turned back to her father. "This unspeakable conduct will never do."

Her father bellowed. "Auralie, I am outraged that you have shamed me like this."

"Covington." Colton grabbed the man by his lapels. "Where is Barnabas?"

"Now see here…" Perry grasped Colton's arm, causing Colton to spin around and land a punch on the side of Perry's jaw, sending him sprawling.

While the men continued to shout at one another, Auralie dashed down the veranda steps and ran toward the back of the house, past the trees, to a clearing that skirted Slave Row. A large group of slaves stood in a wide circle. In the center of the circle was Barnabas, tied to a thick post with his shirt stripped off. One of the overseers approached him, a whip coiled in his hands, announcing to all assembled that the same treatment awaited any of them who tried to run.

"Stop! Stop this!" Auralie screamed at the top of her lungs. She raced toward the horrific scene, screaming as she went. *"Colton!"* She broke through the circle and ran toward Barnabas, gasping for breath and seething with fury. "Stop this, immediately."

The overseer jerked his head, no doubt taken aback at Auralie's presence. "Who are you?"

She stepped in front of Barnabas, drew her shoulders back, and lifted her chin. Her chest heaved as she gulped air. "I am Auralie Covington. This man does not belong to my father. He is not a runaway. I demand you release him at once."

Chapter 18

Amid the bellowing and blustering between Covington and Bolden, Colton realized Auralie no longer stood beside him. He twisted his head to the right and left, searching for her, and caught sight of Mammy standing on the front lawn, pointing frantically toward the back of the house.

At that moment, Auralie's piercing scream rent the air. *"Colton!"*

Colton leaped down the steps.

"Where do you think you're going?" Covington roared.

Bolden staggered to his feet. "Sir, you are a boorish clod, and you will hear from my attorney."

Colton ignored them both and sprinted in the direction Mammy pointed. Another scream reached his ears, and the blood in his veins turned to ice. His heart pounded in his throat as he ran past the stable toward a thick copse of trees. He slid down a steep slope past the trees on a path that opened up to a clearing. Rows of ramshackle hovels lined a rutted road, and the stench of sweat and human waste hung in the air. Dozens of slaves gathered in a circle around the edge of the open area, while in the center of the clearing, a loathsome sight greeted him. Barnabas was tied, with his arms wrapped around a post. An overseer coiled a whip in preparation for use.

But standing between Barnabas and the overseer, hands on her hips and a defiant lift to her jaw, stood Auralie. The vision of her triggered a hitch in his chest, and his breath caught. An exquisite ache filled him as he drank in the valiant picture she made. He moved forward to take his place next to her.

Pounding footsteps sounded behind him, and Bolden called out something about Colton insulting him and he demanded satisfaction. Colton ignored him. The slaves who stood on the fringes of the clearing parted and let Colton slip past.

Auralie looked his way, and the relief in her eyes made him want to take her in his arms. Instead, he let his gaze slide to Barnabas, and acid rage swelled in his chest. He strode, fuming, to the overseer. The man spat tobacco juice at Colton's feet.

Colton grabbed the whip from the man's grimy paw. "I ought to wrap this thing around your worthless neck." He flung it as far as he could into the trees. Barnabas's faded muslin shirt lay on the ground, and Colton bent and snatched it up. He jammed his hand in the pocket and pulled out the indenture paper, unfolded it, and shoved it in the overseer's face.

The man shrugged. "Cain't read."

Colton yanked the bowie knife from the man's belt and went over to cut the ropes holding Barnabas hostage. "Are you all right, my friend?"

Barnabas gave him a wobbly smile despite a swollen lip. "I is now."

Colton folded the paper and handed it, along with the ripped shirt, back to Barnabas before turning to Auralie. Her eyes misted, but she blinked back the moisture.

"Oh Colton. I've never been so glad to see anybody in my entire life."

He held her gaze for a long moment. The tremor in her voice didn't match her bravado, and he longed to whisper in her ear that everything was all right now. He glanced over his shoulder to where Bolden stood fuming, a silk handkerchief pressed over his nose and mouth. This wasn't the time.

The overseer waved his arms and shouted for the workers to get back to their tasks. With eyes held low, they all trudged away while the overseer searched through the trees and underbrush for his whip. Colton's heart ached, but the only thing that would change their circumstances was electing men to office who held to the belief that slavery was immoral.

Shelby Covington approached at a jog, huffing and puffing, his belly jiggling with each footfall.

"Danfield! You're trespassing. Auralie, I'll not permit you to embarrass me any further. Get back to the house this instant."

Auralie folded her arms and turned to face her father with the same expression of confident bravery with which she'd faced the overseer. "No, Father. I am a grown woman, not a child."

Bolden took three strides and grasped Auralie's arm. "I am your future husband, and you'll do as I say."

Colton clamped his hand on Bolden's arm and yanked it away from Auralie, nudging her away from the contemptuous snob. Through gritted teeth, he hissed at Bolden. "You lay a finger on her again, and these folks will have to carry you out of here."

A flinch wavered across Bolden's face, chased into hiding by an expression of indignation.

Shelby Covington barged past Bolden and stood toe-to-toe with Colton. "How dare you come in here and disrupt my daughter's life."

Before Colton could reply, Auralie stepped forward.

"Father, if anyone is disrupting my life, it's you."

Covington's face flooded red and the veins in his neck stood out. He sputtered, but no words formed. But Auralie wasn't finished.

"All my life I've watched you wield your power and authority in such a way that it tramples everyone around you into submission, including Mother and me. It's not my intention to show disrespect to you, but respect can't be demanded." She turned her head and glanced at Colton. "I have far more respect for this man who has dirt under his fingernails and calluses on his hands. He pours his heart and soul and sweat into the land and work God has given him to do. Colton doesn't demand respect. He earns it."

Auralie's words caressed Colton's ears like music. His heart soared.

Bolden, still holding the fancy handkerchief over his face as though he was afraid to breathe the same air as the slaves, looked down his aristocratic nose at Auralie. "Do you have the audacity to insinuate this…this *farmer* appeals to you?" Disbelief echoed in his tone.

A tiny smile tweaked Auralie's lips, and she lifted her gaze to Colton. "Yes. Everything about this man, from his dirty hands and sweaty brow, to the way he asks God to bless him with a good crop, the way he rejoices over a newborn lamb—" She gestured to Barnabas. "And the way he stands up for what is right." She turned her eyes back to

Bolden. "Yes, Colton Danfield appeals to me, Perry. Being forced into an arranged marriage for business and political purposes repulses me."

Bolden's eyes flamed, and then narrowed, first at Auralie, then at Colton. Finally he whirled to confront Covington. "Everything you told me about your daughter is false. She is a most unsuitable match. I will not have a wife who doesn't know her place. You'll be hearing from my attorney regarding the dissolution of our contract." With an incensed snort, he stomped away.

Tears filled Auralie's eyes. She cast a brief glance heavenward, and her lips mouthed the words, *Thank You*.

Colton understood her tears. The sentiment she'd just offered to God flooded his heart as well.

Shelby Covington stood clenching his fist at his sides, his posture domineering. Poison darts of hostility spit from his eyes. "You are to blame for this. I'll see to it my attorney files papers immediately to sue you for every dime you have to your name."

Colton folded his arms across his chest. "I'm glad you have an attorney, Covington, because you're going to need one."

"What?" Covington sent a piercing glare at Colton and cursed. "What are you talking about?"

Colton stroked his chin. "I had a rather interesting conversation with the county clerk at Mount Yonah when I went there several days ago to confirm the deed to my land was properly recorded."

Covington pooched his lips in feigned disinterest and shifted a glance in Auralie's direction. "What does that have to do with me?"

"I can prove that you paid the clerk at the courthouse in Mount Yonah to alter the record ledger."

"That's preposterous!" Covington almost stood on tiptoe as he emitted the bellow. "What kind of pernicious lies are you inventing to besmirch my name?"

Acutely aware of Auralie's eyes upon him, Colton took no pleasure in exposing Covington's misdeeds in her presence, but he suspected she wasn't entirely oblivious to her father's tactics.

The stench of liquor on Shelby Covington's breath nearly turned Colton's stomach, but he faced the man. "Are you denying you paid the county clerk to remove the page in the ledger on which the deed for my land was recorded and to rewrite a new page to replace it?"

Covington sputtered and his face evolved from red to purple. A vein in his temple pulsated visibly. "This is outrageous. You can't accuse me like this, especially when you can't prove a thing."

"Oh, but I can." Colton didn't blink at Covington's bluster. "You see, you forgot something, Covington. Reverend Robert Winslow recorded his will in the same county office, bequeathing his land to me. Pastor Winslow's will and the land deed were recorded at the same time—the deed in one ledger and the will in a different one. A copy of the will is also on file."

"I don't know any Robert Winslow." Moisture beaded on Covington's forehead.

"That's odd, because your son knows about Pastor Winslow. He and I had a conversation one day about three weeks ago when he was out my way doing some surveying. Your son mentioned that I was a landowner only through Pastor Winslow's benevolence."

Covington huffed and stammered. "Y-you... Th–this entire c–conversation is ridiculous."

"You won't think it's ridiculous when you receive a summons from the state attorney general's office." Colton tucked his thumbs into his belt. "Seems the county clerk

wasn't willing to go to jail, so he signed a sworn statement saying you paid him five hundred dollars to change
the ledger pages."

Covington blanched. "He's…he's lying. It was Bolden.
Thaddeus Bolden wanted… He said he'd withdraw his support if…"

"Father, how could you?" Auralie's shocked gasp reminded Colton she was listening to the entire exchange.

Covington turned without another word and plodded up
the slope past the trees. No doubt he'd be penning letters to
Thaddeus Bolden and Maxwell Rayburn within the hour.

Colton watched him until he was beyond the trees.

Colton turned to Auralie and spoke quietly. "I think it's
time for Barnabas and me to leave." Their gazes locked.
He'd not leave her here if she feared her father's wrath. He
tried to sort out the twisted jumble of emotions on her face.
"Will you be all right?"

Some of the starch he'd seen when she stood up to the
overseer, and then to her father and Perry Bolden, seemed
to seep out of her. Her shoulders drooped a bit, but she managed a tight smile. "Yes, for now."

Barnabas pulled his shirt on the best he could—one
sleeve dangled, having been ripped from the shoulder.
"Mistah Colton, I jus' go wait fo' you up yonder." He
bobbed his head toward the rise.

Colton nodded. "Jasper is by the front entrance. He could
probably use some water."

"I see to da hoss. And Mistah Colton, Miz Covington."
He laid his hand over his heart. "I thanks yo' both. I be…
mighty grateful, fo' ever'thin'."

Colton extended his hand and Barnabas gripped it. Then
he stepped back with a polite nod toward Auralie. "Ma'am."
And he hurried away.

Colton placed his hand gently on the small of Auralie's

back, and they slowly made their way together up the pathway that led back to the house. He had so many things on his heart that he wanted to say to her, but getting the words to line up in an order that would make sense suddenly seemed a daunting task. He drew in a deep breath and released it.

"Auralie, how can I thank you for what you did?"

She angled her head and peered up at him, her demure smile nearly doing him in. "What did I do?"

"You showed remarkable courage in the way you stopped that overseer." He took her elbow and turned her to him. "I think I understand a little of what it took for you to stand up to your father after being subjected to his intimidation for so many years." He glanced down at his boots. "I'm sorry you had to hear all those things I said to him."

She touched his hand and a tremble skittered up his arm. "Colton, I'm sorry for what my father did, or tried to do. He wasn't always that way—so filled with greed he'd sell his soul to gain more power. He used to care more for my mother and me. I don't know why or how he changed." She sighed.

They continued walking, passing the stable and entering the sprawling side yard with its majestic magnolia trees and lush rhododendrons. Colton spied Mammy watching them from an upstairs window. She gave Colton a smile and a nod, quite the opposite of his first meeting with Auralie. He couldn't help but grin.

Auralie stopped and sat on an ornate, wrought iron bench among the roses. "I don't understand why Father tried to change the land records."

Colton sat beside her. "Jack McCaffey was the one who suggested I go and check the records. His sources told him there was a deal in the works to bring the Georgia Railroad spur up this way from Athens. Thaddeus Bolden bought a thousand acres of timberland that borders my property, and the shortest route to access the spur extension was through my land. He knew I wouldn't sell, and one of Jack's sources got wind of some under-the-table dealing at the county seat. When Jack saw a map of the tentative route for the spur, he told me about it."

Auralie closed her eyes and nodded. "Thaddeus Bolden is Father's biggest financial supporter."

"That's right." Colton cupped his hands over his knees. "Your father could win the election on Bolden's wallet, and once in office, he'd be Bolden's puppet for political favors—like seizing possession of land that didn't have a properly recorded deed."

Auralie covered her face with her hands. "Oh Colton, I'm so sorry…"

"There's no need for you to be sorry." He slipped his fingers around her wrists and tugged her hands away from her beautiful face. A chuckle bubbled up within him. The wild carriage ride had pulled pins from her hair and set the sandy tendrils in disarray, and she had a smudge of dirt on her face, but she was still the prettiest thing he'd ever seen. He brushed back a lock of her hair, and she pressed her head against his knuckles.

"Did you really mean what you said about being glad to see me?"

A rosy blush stole into her cheeks, and her eyes twinkled. "Yes."

Colton cleared his throat. "Well, then, there's something I'd like to say to you, but I'm not sure if this is the right time, or even if I'm the right person."

She dropped her gaze to her lap. Colton reached over and took her hand. She blinked and raised her eyes to meet his. "First I must ask your forgiveness for misjudging you. The day I met you, I assumed you were a spoiled, self-centered young woman who only cared about herself. I happily admit I was wrong."

Surprise flickered across her face. "Why did you think that?"

Colton shook his head. "The reasons aren't important. What matters is that God gave me the privilege of truly getting to know you. I think I was smitten the day you brought the lemonade to Barnabas and me." He grinned when she blushed. "I knew I had lost my heart to you the morning we worked together helping birth the twin lambs."

A shy smile graced her lips. "That was special to me, too."

"A little while ago, you said you respected me for having dirty hands and calluses from working." He hesitated and searched her face. "I have to know if you said that simply to offend Bolden."

Her wide, solemn eyes answered him even before she spoke. "No, Colton, I meant every word. The Bible says a man ought to work with his hands and care for those things the Lord has given him. That's what you do. How can I not respect that?"

Colton pulled in a slow, deep breath. His heart thrummed within his chest. "Auralie, I believe with all my heart that when God created a helpmate for me, He had you in mind."

Her eyes misted, and she gifted him with that endearing smile he'd come to adore. "I believe that, too."

He slid off the bench to one knee, capturing both her hands in his. "Auralie, I love you with all my heart. I'm asking you to be my wife."

"Yes, Colton. With all my heart, I want to marry you."

Epilogue

September 1860

Auralie looked at the house as if she'd never seen it before as Colton drove up to the front and reined in the team. The meeting in town with Lloyd and Belle at Cyrus Fletcher's office had been a celebration, topped off with lunch at Maybelle's Café. The only sad part was the good-bye, and even that was sprinkled with giggles as Belle's swollen stomach got in the way of their hugs and promises to write once Belle got settled in their new house in Atlanta.

"Colton, I'm still pinching myself to make sure this isn't a dream." Auralie could barely contain her excitement. "I spent many joy-filled days in this house last spring."

He lifted her down from the wagon and gave her a peck on her nose. "We will make sure a lot more joy abides with us in the coming days, Mrs. Danfield."

Soft laughter bubbled up from her throat and accompanied a warm flush at hearing her new name. Colton took her hand.

"I want to show you something." They rounded the corner of the house to the side porch swathed in afternoon shade from the stately oaks. There sat the wicker chairs with their colorful cushions and the small table where Auralie and Belle had enjoyed midmorning tea or afternoon lemonade while they talked out the issues they faced.

"Belle left them here for you as a belated wedding gift."

Auralie released a soft gasp and clapped both hands over her chest. "But she and Lloyd already gave us that lovely quilt." She climbed the two steps up to the wide wraparound porch and picked up a book from the chair she'd occupied so many pleasant hours. Amusement tickled her stomach. "*Wuthering Heights*. I never did finish it. Look, she even left my bookmark in place."

"I'm afraid the furnishings will be a bit sparse for a while." Colton joined her on the porch. "Lloyd and Belle took most of the furniture with them. You'll be happy to know they left the bookshelves in the parlor."

Auralie ran her hand over the railing, still in awe the house was now theirs. "Oh look, there's Barnabas." She waved at the man working in the meadow, and he reciprocated. "What is he doing?"

Colton slipped his arm around his bride. "With the purchase of the house and land, we're able to expand the sheep pasture to include four more acres, so Barnabas is working on new fencing."

She looked out across the meadow and imagined the sheep grazing there as soon as Barnabas finished the fence. "What did he say when you told him he'd be living in the cabin now instead of the lean-to?"

Colton grinned. "I didn't tell him." He gave her a sly wink. "I showed him. I wrote it out for him to read. His face lit up like a sunrise. I think he was more excited that he could read it for himself than he was about living in the cabin."

Ripples of delight darted through her. She stepped toward the door that opened to the side porch.

"Where do you think you're going, Mrs. Danfield?"

She pointed. "Can't we go inside?"

A wide grin poked a dimple in her husband's cheek. "Not until I carry you over the threshold." He scooped her into his arms.

"Colton! We've been married almost two months, and we've visited Lloyd and Belle here at least a dozen times as husband and wife." But she snuggled against his shoulder and enjoyed the closeness.

"Ah, but now the house is ours, and a proper husband should carry his wife across the threshold." He lowered his lips to hers. "Are you sure you don't mind that we didn't have the big fancy wedding you would have had with Perry Bolden?"

"Oh Colton, it's not the wedding that's important. It's the marriage." She buried her face in his neck. "God has given me a most priceless gift—the best husband I could ever imagine."

He nudged the door with his shoulder, and it swung open with no effort.

A voice, nearly as familiar as her own, greeted them. "Welcome home, honey girl."

"Mammy!"

Colton set her down and she embraced her dear friend. "What are you doing here?" She looked back at her husband, expecting a mischievous grin, but he appeared as surprised as she.

Mammy pulled a paper from her apron pocket and handed it to Auralie. "Never thought I'd see the day that yo' mama would stand up strong to yo' daddy, but tha's jus' what she done. She talk yo' daddy into signin' me ovah to you, as a weddin' present."

Astonishment dropped Auralie's jaw. "Mother did that?"

"Yes she did. Yo' daddy did some hollerin', but yo' mama got her way." Mammy winked. "Sho' s'prise me, too. But I's mighty happy to be here, takin' care o' my honey girl, again." She leaned close to Auralie and whispered. "An' maybe I gets to take care o' yo' babies, too."

A rush of heat filled Auralie's face. "Maybe sooner than you think." She looked up into Colton's widened eyes.

"What?"

"I've been sick to my stomach three mornings in a row." Mammy clapped her hands and cackled. "Halleluiah!"

* * * * *